A MEASURE OF TIME

GILLIAN JACKSON

BLOODHOUND
— BOOKS —

www.bloodhoundbooks.com

Print ISBN: 978-1-916978-98-0

To everything there is a season, a time for every purpose under Heaven.
A time to be born, and a time to die... A time to weep, and a time to laugh.
— Ecclesiastes, Chapter 3

PROLOGUE
MEGAN, 2019

Only after her death did I find Mum's journal, perched rather prominently on the edge of the huge family dining table where we'd enjoyed so many wonderful occasions. It was the only thing out of place in an otherwise immaculate dining room, so I assumed she wanted me to find it and idly thumbed through the pages. A single loose sheet fell to the floor, and as I picked it up, the sight of Mum's small neat handwriting once again prompted the awful raw feeling of loss. Taking the letter and journal to the sofa, I tucked my legs up to warm my cold feet and began reading.

> To my dearest Luke and Megan,
> If you are reading this, then I have already left you, not by choice, but I have accepted my fate and am ready to go.
> You're probably wondering why I'm writing this journal. The answer is for you, but also for myself. Over the last few years, I've found writing to be therapeutic and a great way to rationalise those crazy, intrusive

thoughts which make me restless by day and an insomniac by night. It has become a discipline, a tool to keep me grounded and, more importantly, to stop myself from falling into the pit of self-pity, to keep from asking the question 'Why me?' and instead to wonder 'Why not me?' I suppose this could be described as a journal, a diary of events recorded in retrospect and read frequently enough to preserve my sanity and bring perspective into my strange, somewhat limited new world. (There are perhaps a few plans which may or may not come to fruition.)

In this brief and hastily added prelude to my scribbles, I'd ask your forgiveness for any negativity on these pages. If I appear to be rambling, please blame the medication – I know, it's a pretty lame excuse!

For my wonderful wider family and friends, let these words be a comfort and a benediction to the strength of our bond, and please, know that I love you all more than life itself. Many of you have shared the dark times with me, yet to recognise the dark, we must also have light, so I ask you to remember the brilliant sun-filled times we've shared. I hope where our lives have touched, you will remember me for good rather than evil and forgive the failings I've made along the way – we are all weak sometimes.

And to my children, you have been nothing less than a delight to your father and me, and my hope is that you will live your lives to the full, making the most of each day, each moment, for time is so precious, yet unfathomable – an unknown quantity. Leaving this

account of my life with you may be a risk, but I'm
hoping you might learn from my mistakes and be able to
forgive my frailties. Keep strong and live your lives with
compassion and love.
   Your loving mother,
   Helen.

I've always been proud to call Helen Reid my mother and
naively assumed my twin brother Luke and I knew everything
there was to know about her. It appears we were mistaken. I
suppose all children must think a parent's life only begins when
they are born, and it's only as they grow into maturity that it
dawns on them their parents are real people too, with a past
their offspring may know little about. This certainly proved true
for me, and the real Helen Reid, the woman rather than the
mother and grandmother I knew, was to be found in her own
words in the form of the book I held in my hand.

Mum was taken from us far too soon, as was my father,
Andrew, three years ago. Although she repeatedly told us she
was ready to go, I wasn't prepared to let go of her. Reluctantly
we accepted Mum's decisions about her illness and treatment as
her right, even though we found it hard to bear. Luke and I were
with her at the end, the three of us holding hands across the soft
lemon duvet, forming an unbroken triangle in the private room
of the hospice which had done so much for us all. As her last
breath escaped from between thin, pale lips, I could swear those
same lips curled into a contented smile. We at least had time to
say goodbye, which wasn't the case with Dad, who was taken so
suddenly.

The letter intrigued me, and I was keen to read the journal
as soon as possible, but I was in Mum's house for a purpose – to
clear the last of her possessions, not to read and reflect. I tucked

the book carefully into my bag, resisting the urge to delve into its pages immediately, and moved into the bedroom to pack her clothes. They were to go to the local hospice shop to support their work, a meagre gesture of thanks for the care Mum received from them. There were only a couple of hours for me to complete the task before someone from the shop called to pick up the bags.

I worked quickly; the house had been cold but was slowly warming up. I must remember to set the heating to fire up with regularity in order to air the rooms. A house can soon feel cold and neglected if left empty for long. Strangely the place seemed different already and I felt no pull or sentiment there, probably due to Mum's pragmatic attitude and the myriad instructions left with us regarding her earthly possessions.

Inevitably some of Mum's clothes brought back memories of our shared history; the pale-blue suit she wore for my wedding hung in the back of the wardrobe, protected by a polythene garment cover. A couple of hat boxes nestled on the top shelf, containing the only two hats Mum possessed, a neat little blue one she'd also worn for my wedding and a white, wide-brimmed affair she bought for Luke and Imogen's wedding. Both were worn only once; she was not a hat person and needed to be almost bullied into buying them by Dad.

There was little more to pack, Mum had sorted the clothes herself, and only the best was left for the charity shop. I was starting to realise exactly how much effort she'd put into dismantling her life, typically preparing well to make things as easy as possible for those of us who were left behind.

My task was completed just as the collection van arrived promptly at three. I helped to carry some of the bags while the driver, an elderly volunteer with a permanent smile on his ruddy face, who mumbled 'thank you' at least a thousand times, lifted the boxes which were set aside and neatly labelled.

There was no more to do for the present, but before locking the door, I walked around each room in turn, starting upstairs. The master bedroom had remained unchanged since my father died. My husband, James, offered to decorate it several times, but Mum always politely refused. I think this was where she felt closest to Dad. They'd chosen the decor and furnishings together, and I understood why she wished it to remain untouched. Mum struggled to come to terms with Dad's death, and it had taken over a year for her to sort out his clothes, even though I offered to help on several occasions.

Upstairs were three more bedrooms, the smallest used as a study for my father, and the other two were once mine and Luke's. All three rooms were virtually unchanged from when I lived at home, except for fresh paint on the walls and new bedding. Standing in my old room felt rather weird. Memories of my childhood filled the space – I pictured myself with toys and teddy bears as a little girl, then later as a teenager sitting at the tiny desk doing homework or playing loud music until asked by one or other of my parents to turn it down. I spent only a minute or two in Luke's room. Although redecorated in recent years, it was still very much a boy's room. Here we'd hatched wicked childhood pranks, sitting cross-legged on the floor and laughing crazily as we dared each other to carry them out, which, thankfully, we rarely did.

I trudged downstairs on weary legs, with hardly a glance into the study, bare now with the hundreds of Dad's books given away and only dust replacing them on the shelves.

The bright, modern kitchen looked as pristine as the day it was fitted. This was one of the few changes Mum made after Dad died and was probably only done as a project to occupy her thoughts. The estate agent almost drooled over the quality fitments and declared this and the large modern bathroom to be 'great selling points'. From the window, most of the garden was visible and I blinked rapidly as the image of a pigtailed child, laughing and swinging higher and higher on the garden swing came to mind. Had I stayed much longer, there would have been many other memories of happy, carefree times with my brother and parents, but it was time to leave.

I locked the door, carefully avoiding looking at the 'For Sale' board standing at a precarious angle in the front garden, and headed home. My mind was already anticipating what I might discover in the journal, mentally questioning what Mum's alleged *failings* could be. On reaching home, pausing only to boil the kettle and make a much-needed coffee, I turned up the heating, opened the book and started to read.

ONE
THE JOURNAL

3rd August 2017

My name is Helen Reid, and today is a memorable day, one which has changed my status from a fully functioning human being to a struggling one, from having a future to complete and utter uncertainty. It is the day when I embark on my final journey.

Sitting outside the consultant's office at Castleford Hospital was not somewhere I'd choose to be on such a promising August morning. Yet the past few weeks have been a whirl of such appointments, from GP to consultant, to scans and blood tests, and other procedures I wouldn't care to describe here. But this was the big one – the day I'd receive the verdict – the results of a recent biopsy.

My wait was unusually short, perhaps a bad omen, and when Mr Connors popped his head into the corridor, seeking me out, I knew the news was not good. The consultant's expression was one of practised sympathy, features arranged as per the gravity of the news about to be delivered. His forehead was furrowed, eyebrows almost meeting across his nose, like a caterpillar underlining his brow. Thin lips pressed tightly together, parted only to deliver the verdict.

I heard only some of his words, *ovarian cancer, stages, grades*, too many words to process, and my mind switched to other thoughts. Did he practise his 'bad news' face in front of the mirror to ensure he got it right? A sudden rush of sympathy for the man washed over me. It must be terrible to regularly tell patients their condition was terminal, even with treatment. As more of his words snagged in my mind, *aggressive cancer, chemotherapy, surgery, so sorry*, Mr Robert Connors reached for my hand, covering it with his own.

'Has anyone come with you today, Helen?'

I lifted my eyes to meet his – soft brown eyes with flecks of yellow around the iris, kind, puppy-dog eyes filled with genuine empathy. I forced a smile and shook my head; this was still my secret, to share only when I was ready. Mr Connors scribbled on a paper, handed it to me, and asked me to make another appointment on my way out to discuss treatment, and he suggested a family member accompany me next time. He then placed a rather large file with my name on it into a tray on his desk. I wondered if it was the *hopeless* tray.

I am fifty-nine years old and currently living on borrowed time. Mr Connors has confirmed it, so it's official. It is doubtful whether I shall reach my sixtieth birthday, and barring a miracle, it is a given that the allotted three score and ten is not to be my portion. Leaving the hospital building to seek out my car in the vast, sprawling car park, I wondered if I should ask someone to accompany me next time, but who? Megan is the obvious choice. If Andrew were still alive, there would be no doubt he would hold my hand for every step of this journey. But my husband is dead, and I own the most awful of labels, *widow*. It appears I have spent my life collecting labels, *wife, daughter, mother of twins, grandmother, friend, retiree, widow,* and now the most universally feared label of all, *cancer sufferer*.

Instead of driving straight home, I headed north, where, within a few miles, the stunning West Yorkshire countryside enfolded me in its beauty, so close to my home and heart. It had been an early appointment and the sun was only just breaking through the morning cloud, bringing its welcome warmth to the air. Stopping in a lay-by and switching off the engine, I stepped out of the car to draw deep breaths of the clean, invigorating air. Everything appeared sharp and clear, the distant green hills dotted liberally with trees and shrubs and the pure white of the puffy clouds – a beautiful powder-blue sky peeping between them, promising another lovely day. But was the scene really so vivid, or was I simply seeing it through different eyes, having been granted the clarity that comes with knowing you will soon be leaving this world? Time, however, was not about to stand still to afford me the luxury of breathing in this scene indefinitely, and I must return home.

10th August

Perhaps it's natural for my thoughts to be focused so much on Andrew lately. He was the love of my life, my soulmate. Corny, maybe, but we completed each other, laughed at the same things, finished each other's sentences and shared a life as near perfect as anyone's could be.

A few months before Andrew died, we watched a re-run of the film *The Bucket List* on television and laughed at the antics of Jack Nicholson and Morgan Freeman as they attempted to cram a lifetime of living into a measured span of time before their respective deaths from cancer. Although light-hearted, it was one of those films which made an impact and prompted thoughts of what we would do in a similar situation. The conversation began with a discussion on whether it was preferable to know you were about to die or not. This topic is not nearly as much fun as the 'What would you do if you won the lottery?' question, but the sad reality is that the lottery win is far less likely to happen. Our thoughts on the former issue were in accord, as Andrew and I agreed that going to bed one night and simply not waking up was the preferred way to go. I even remember rolling my eyes heavenward and saying, *Please, God*, with absolute sincerity.

Because we were so alive and vital then, death could be discussed casually and with a degree of humour. I was the grand old age of fifty-six and Andrew a more elderly fifty-nine. We assumed we'd knock around for years to come, living the dream. Our grown-up twins, Megan and Luke, were happily settled with their partners, and Megan with our son-in-law James, had presented us with our first adorable grandchild, Sam, upon whom we naturally doted. Financially we were rock solid, having spent thirty years building up a haulage firm from the humble beginnings of one vehicle to a fleet of nearly forty. At the time, we were negotiating to sell out to a large international company, after which we planned to travel and enjoy life. Perhaps we'd buy a second home somewhere in the country where our family could join us for holidays – an idyllic life rolled out before us into an endless ribbon of warm summers and crisp white winters. Chestnuts roasting and all that. But it was not meant to be.

Andrew was taken from us within weeks of seeing the film. His wish of going to sleep and not waking up was granted, but it was early, far too early. And while it may be an excellent way to die, it's a cruel and shattering blow to those left behind. Pulling together as a family, we knew life would change dramatically without Andrew. He was a vibrant, larger-than-life personality whose passing left a massive void in our midst. How could I go on? I'd forgotten what life was like being single. My very identity was as one half of a couple. It was all I knew how to be.

The loss was so brutally painful and raw, and even now, there are times I still feel rudderless, having lost my one true love, my entirety, my rock. It's almost three years ago – Andrew died on a bleak November night, totally unexpected, the victim of an aneurysm which could not have been predicted. To wake up beside the love of your life to discover him cold and dead is one colossal shock. Initially, I was paralysed with fear and then found myself shaking Andrew violently, shouting at him to wake up, although I knew in my heart my husband was gone.

It was final, brutal. He would never again solve all my problems, be there to hold and comfort me and make me laugh in the unique way he had when I took life too seriously. Never again would Andrew gently touch my cheek, make love to me, or make me feel special and wanted.

Over the following months, our children were fantastic. Although mourning a much-loved father, their grief was put on hold in an attempt to help me through those dark, wretched days. Thankfully the sale of the business went through without a hitch. Yet without Andrew by my side, there was no joy in planning the future and no work to immerse myself in either. I tried so hard to be a glass-half-full person and count the blessings in life which remained, but it was achingly impossible. I struggled to get through the days, and then inevitably, the lonely nights closed around me to remind me of my heart's emptiness and my cold bed. Even though it's been nearly three years, a vacant, hollow feeling remains. I miss my husband more than words can describe.

Luke moved to Canada the year before Andrew died. Knowing his plans to seek a new life for his family, we attempted to encourage him, pushing our selfish sadness to the back of our minds. I refused to make it difficult for my son to move on – they must do what was right and follow their dream. But it was so hard to be genuinely happy for them. Within months of their move, our daughter-in-law, Imogen, gave birth to a son, Ethan, and before Andrew's death, we'd planned to visit them in Canada and meet the grandson we'd only ever seen images of in photographs or on Skype. But it wasn't to be, and I felt bereft with the two men in my life no longer there for me.

Luke came over for the funeral while Imogen remained home with Ethan, the little boy Andrew would never meet. My son's presence, albeit only temporary, brought Megan and me a degree of comfort. Still, we knew he would return to his family and I tried hard to suppress the stab of jealousy I felt for no longer being the most significant woman in Luke's life.

During the next few months, I moped and wallowed in self-pity. Some days it was an effort to even get out of bed and dress. The pain was almost physical at times, but I pasted on my smile and heard those I love whisper how well I was coping. Inside I was screaming, but letting my feelings show would do no good for anyone. Luke returned home a week after the funeral, leaving Megan to pick up the pieces and do her best to set me right. It was probably for her, James and Sam that I began to rebuild my shattered life.

Sam was a year old, and his world was one of excitement, exploration, and pure joy. As a family, they were there for me when I needed them, and eventually, I began to put things into perspective and come out of the awful fog of self-pity. I'd been blind to Megan and Luke's pain, so deeply rooted in my own sorrow, but the time came to put away the aching sense of loss and dwell on the good things in my life, of which I still had plenty – to again become the mother and grandmother my family deserved.

My GP referred me to a bereavement counsellor, a lovely

lady whom I eventually discovered was also a widow. She offered a non-judgemental ear, tolerated my angst, and helped me face the pain I had locked away inside. With her wisdom and help, I started to move forward and etch out a new life, not one I would have chosen, but one forced on me with Andrew's death. It was also her suggestion to write a journal, and writing became strangely cathartic, a release of pent-up emotions and a way of charting my progress in coming to terms with Andrew's death.

In the spring after his death, I took great delight in burning my first journal's rambling, negative words. Symbolically, this was the beginning of my new life. Yes, it would always be tinged with sadness as I learned to live with the pain of missing Andrew, but by then, I could focus on the good memories we'd shared and on the family we'd created in our union of love. It was a conscious decision to stop writing the journal, and destroying it heralded a new, more positive phase.

Yet life has a habit of turning your world upside down, almost laughing at the confidence and arrogance of positive thinking and future planning and throwing chaos back into the mix. Another blow to our family was heading in our direction in the form of a greatly feared word, *cancer*. Isn't it ironic that the last crucial decisions I shall make in this life are concerning my death? This is not what I anticipated or planned, but as death is the only certainty in life, I must accept its inevitability. There's no other choice.

This time I'll be prepared – with the chance to plan the last months of my life, I will do so with positivity, with my family in mind, and hopefully, ease the pain they will experience at another loss. Again, I have turned to a journal, but this time, knowing its value and therapeutic powers, I'll continue to use this tool for as long as possible. If you're reading this, Megan and Luke, I hope you will accept the mistakes I've made for what they are. Whether caused by poor judgement, lack of vision or simple cowardice, it's impossible to say, as impossible as correcting every wrong move made in weakness, or for reasons which now seem pathetic. Perhaps you can learn from my mistakes. Who knows? But my greatest desire is for you to remember me fondly and find it in your heart to overlook my human frailties.

TWO
HELEN

12th August

The dream visited me again last night, the same one which haunted me throughout my late teens, and once again I experienced an awful familiar cocktail of panic and guilt surging through my body like an electric current. Suddenly I was back in the car with Rob on the most terrifying night of my life, going far too fast, dangerously so. I was afraid and trembling, but Rob laughed at my pleas to slow down, pushing the car to go even faster, arrogant in his ability to control the machine. Trees and fields blurred into a continuous streak of autumn russets and golds, caught in the headlights as we sped past them. I gripped tightly to the edge of the seat, utterly helpless.

I awoke soaked with perspiration and breathing rapidly. Throwing off the covers and making my way to the bathroom I tried to wash the nightmare away in a frantic, hot shower. A futile exercise – there was a reason the dream had returned and I could ignore it no longer. Having reached a watershed, I was embarking on a quest to relive some of the best memories of my life, but this nightmare, the very worst memory, was refusing to let me go. Do I also have to address this issue to achieve peace, and how can I possibly do so? Surely, it's too late, and where on earth would I begin? Pushing it to the back of my mind, I dressed, went downstairs to make coffee and toast, and then booted up my laptop, notepad ready, to search for flights to Canada.

It's an old trick, filling up your mind with positive thoughts, attempting to edge out the unpleasant, niggling ones you don't wish to acknowledge or address. It occasionally works but sadly, not today. Shuddering as I focused on flight times and prices, trying to find the best travel time didn't fully occupy my thoughts but I pressed on. It was imperative to travel as soon as possible to say goodbye to my son and his family. Naturally, it will be a shock for them, but it is hardly something to disclose on Skype, especially if the connection is inadequate, as it often is, and images keep breaking up.

After making notes of a few possible dates, I stared at the screen, wondering what else I could do on the laptop to keep my mind busy. Facebook's always good for procrastination, so I logged into my rarely-used account to see what my friends were up to. The newsfeed was full of holiday snaps and plans to get away. I typed a few comments, wishing my friends a wonderful summer and briefly mentioned I planned to visit Luke in Canada. I rarely posted on my page, never knowing what to say and not having the snappy vocabulary people used on Facebook. I couldn't bring myself to call everyone 'hun' and to type 'lol', whatever it means. I was probably one of the few who used punctuation in their posts or checked for spelling mistakes before posting.

Procrastination finished, my mind turned back to the nightmare. I wanted to make my own bucket list of things to do and places to visit while still able, but the nightmare had reminded me it was not only the good times I must revisit. The past held unresolved issues, and I was reluctantly nudged into considering again those events which brought such ignominy when they occurred, and even now held the power to unsettle my thoughts and make me sick with those awful memories which I can never fully shake off.

It's also time to tell Megan of my illness. I have an appointment to see Mr Connors again soon and want to ask my daughter to come with me. Over the last few weeks, she's guessed I'm unwell but accepted my lame excuses of hay fever, coupled with missing Andrew during the holiday season. Also, I need to outline my plans to go to Canada and ask Megan to keep my health problems to herself until I have the opportunity to tell Luke face to face.

My poor Megan, I knew it wouldn't be easy and how distressed she would be. This is one of those awful times when, as a mother, I longed to make things better for my daughter but was utterly powerless to do so. It would take more than a mother's hug and sympathetic wisdom to make the situation right for my daughter.

I chose a time when Megan would be at home and Sam at nursery. Telephoning first, I tried to sound upbeat and asked her to put the kettle on as I was coming over. The coffee, however, remained untouched on the kitchen table as I shared the grim news. After absorbing the reality that I was suffering from cancer, my daughter reached out to me and sobbed on my shoulder. I held her for what seemed an age until the tears dried up and Megan was composed enough to ask questions.

Firstly, she asked about possible treatment, a diplomatic way to phrase what she wanted to know, which was, is it terminal? I'd taken in enough of the consultant's words to understand that any treatment would only slightly prolong life, giving a few more weeks or at best months, so yes, it was undoubtedly terminal. My darling Megan, I can hardly bear to see the hurt in your eyes and hope there's enough time to help you prepare for what is to come. I'll tell you my decision regarding treatment later. The knowledge of my body being invaded by cancer is enough for one day. We'll talk again soon, when hopefully I shall help you understand what even I don't fully understand myself.

———

18th August

As I write, Gus is curled up at my feet, occasionally whining to remind me of his presence and how much he would like to go for his walk. Gus is my new best friend, a dog of dubious pedigree who arrived at my door by accident, or at least this is what I'm supposed to believe. He turned up with Megan a few weeks after Andrew died, wrapped in a blanket and wearing one of those ridiculous-looking collars to prevent him from gnawing at a wound on his leg. My daughter is a veterinary nurse and cannot escape from the practice she loves, even on weekends off. The story she told was of Gus being brought in after an injury in a road accident, and with no microchip, his owners could not be found. Perhaps it was a set-up, but I didn't mind. Gus wheedled his way into my heart with a single, doe-eyed look. Although initially timid, which was understandable after his experience, I agreed to foster him until his owners were traced. It took only a week for me to realise I didn't want his owners to be found, and after a month, I had him microchipped as mine, and we settled down into our quiet domestic routine.

Gus gives me purpose, even if it is just walking through the park in all weathers, and a purpose is good, exactly what I needed and what Megan had so transparently planned. Of course, a dog cannot replace a husband, but he's faithful and affectionately sweet, so, despite my good intentions, Gus has filled the cold spot on my bed. He's even patient with Sam, who chases him around each time he visits. Gus is the first dog I've owned and it works. We're a team. It's only a week now until I begin my journey to Canada, so he'll be cared for by Megan, aided by an enthusiastic Sam. I hope my poor dog will retain his patience, but I'm sure he'll find a quiet corner to escape Sam's attention when necessary.

Megan will also take on the responsibility of visiting her grandmother, who currently lives in a nursing home for the elderly. This is the first time I can see my mother's illness as a blessing. Alzheimer's is such a cruel disease, robbing its victims of their dignity whilst their loved ones can do nothing other than watch the progress of the disease as it takes them away, piece by piece. At least my mother will not have to face losing her only child before her time is spent and will be happily oblivious when I am no longer around.

If I recall correctly, it was on Mum's seventy-fifth birthday when we knew the disease had taken hold – at a rather posh restaurant we took her to. When the soup was served, she took out her false teeth to put them on the pristine white linen tablecloth, and I thought the waiter would pass out. Andrew turned bright red with embarrassment whilst Megan and Luke couldn't stop laughing. (Do you remember, Megan?) As ever, Mum was oblivious to it all, but the day served to spur us on to action for her own safety. The disease rapidly claimed more and more of my mother, and now she rarely recognises any of her family and needs constant supervision.

I've spoken to Luke a few times over the last week. He's concerned about me travelling alone and suggested I ask a friend to accompany me. A generous offer on his part, but of course, my son doesn't yet know the reason for my visit, and taking a friend is certainly not appropriate on this occasion. Luke and Imogen have been planning this 'holiday', and it appears I shall see some of their adopted home country. Megan too is worried about me travelling alone. It will be the first time I've been abroad without Andrew, but there are worse things I'll have to do in the coming months, which may even help to toughen me up. I'll be away for a little over two weeks. Luke tried to persuade me to stay longer, which generally I would have done, but there are other things to attend to; time has become a very precious commodity as I'm unsure how much more of it I have.

THREE
RACHEL

I cannot remember a time in my life when I didn't want to become a nurse; it seems to have been my goal almost from day one. Some might say it was in my blood. I have many other early memories, including being in day-care while my mother, Martha Walters, worked as a full-time typist in an office in town. Mostly, those days were happy times when I learned to share with other children, take turns on the swings, and make model palaces from cardboard boxes, shiny tin foil, copious amounts of glue and pink paint. But a handful of bad memories also seem to have lodged in my mind. A fall from the climbing frame in the nursery garden necessitated a visit to the hospital for stitches, and as my mother couldn't be contacted, one of the staff comforted me when it was my mum I wanted. (Perhaps this early hospital visit related to my desire to be a nurse?) Being made to eat everything on the plate at dinner time was another not-so-good memory which has snagged in my mind for some reason. But the best memories, however, are of those times when Mum didn't have to go to work – when we were free to be together and do anything we wished – long carefree days, ending after tea time with her brushing the tangle of my red, unruly hair before stories and bedtime.

Our holidays amounted to day trips to the coast on a train. I loved the rhythm of the train on its tracks and would hum along to the cadence or make up words to sing. We would make spectacular sandcastles on the beach, running back and forth to the sea to collect water for the moat. Even now, the memories can elicit the feel of warm gritty sand between my toes. There were impromptu picnics in the local park and games in our home's tiny garden, which frequently involved playing nurses. My dolls and teddies were rarely found without bandages, and I dosed Mum with 'medicine' from plastic bottles, which I insisted would make her feel much better. Yes, they were simple pleasures but exciting to a young child, and in my mind's eye, the sun always shone high in the sky, the birds sang sweetly and the grass was rich and green. Mum taught me to make daisy chains, and as we walked through the woods, we collected wild flowers to press between the pages of my story books to dry. We'd then mount them in scrapbooks with their names printed neatly underneath. Buttercups, bluebells, coltsfoot, shepherd's purse; I knew them all. Life was simple and I never felt in the least deprived. My mother made sure of that.

By the age of eight or nine, I became aware of the differences between me and the other children at school, and one day I asked my mother why she went to work every day when my friends had mothers who stayed at home and had their tea ready after school. She pulled me onto her knee and tried to explain.

'I need to go to work to earn money for us to live. We need food, clothes, and our little treats, which all take money.'

'But why don't we get a daddy? Then he could go to work, and you could stay home and bake cakes?' It was a simple question but almost impossible for Mum to answer or for me to understand. I knew I had a daddy once – there was a photograph on the dresser of him and Mummy on their wedding day, but he'd gone away, and now there were just the two of us.

'We can't just get a daddy, Rachel, you know it's not so simple. Although – perhaps if there was a daddy shop, we could go and buy one!' She tickled me until we rolled onto the floor, laughing until I needed to pee and the subject was closed or at least evaded for the time being. Martha Walters was a remarkable woman who worked hard to provide a decent life for us both, a life with which we were content and happy in the love we shared.

School days were brilliant and carefree, and I thrived on learning. At secondary school, the teachers predicted I'd go far. Naturally, my mother was proud and saved whatever she could manage from her meagre earnings to give me choices and to allow me to follow my dream when the time came.

When I was old enough to be safely left at home alone, my mother took on a second job cleaning offices two evenings a week, the money from which went straight into the university fund. Finishing the last year of secondary school as Head Girl with top grades in all my chosen subjects, I think my mother was more excited than I was. We celebrated by treating ourselves to a weekend in London, a rare and exciting event that we both thoroughly enjoyed. Together we wandered around Covent Garden, breathing in the carnival atmosphere and watching street performers entertaining the public. I worked in a bakery each Saturday morning and managed to save enough money to buy tickets for *The Lion King*. The show was a fitting end to our weekend away, a colourful, magical experience unlike anything we'd ever seen before and an event which would stay in our minds for a long time to come.

The summer was a bittersweet time for both Mum and me.

We'd never been apart, and although going to university had long been our joint goal, it precipitated a change in our lives which would not be easy.

My ambition was still to become a nurse, although my teachers said I could easily set my sights higher and aim to be a doctor, but true to my heart, nursing it was. So, with excellent grades in GCSEs and four good 'A' levels, I was accepted at De Montfort University Leicester to study adult nursing, with a view to a degree in palliative care. It would be four years of training, in theory at the university and practice at various placements, and I was under no illusion it would be easy.

Student nurses started on the bottom rung of the ladder, from bedpans to enemas – definitely not for the faint-hearted. However, with Leicester being my chosen university and not a million miles from home, keeping in touch would be relatively easy, a fact Mum and I both appreciated.

I took to the studies like the proverbial duck to water, thriving on the academic content of the training and sensibly pacing the work. After three months of lectures and assignments, we were finally let loose on the hospital wards, encountering various illnesses and conditions in the general medical wards and learning how to interact with patients. The latter came naturally, having always had a heart for people and a desire to help in every possible way.

During the first year, I lived in halls at the university, in a cramped room furnished sparsely with a bed, a single wardrobe, a desk and a sink. Bathroom facilities were shared by residents of the whole corridor, as were washing machines and irons. It was adequate, and as meals were provided on campus, there was little I needed to buy. I shared a house with two other girls for the following three years. As rentals go, it was clean and cheap, and we had our own rooms, a sanctuary for study and sleep, with shared bathroom and kitchen facilities. Fortunately, I got on well with my housemates, primarily because we were all so busy working shifts or studying, and all three of us in the house together at any time was rare.

On my weekends off or rest days after shift work, I went home as often as possible to share my new life and experiences with Mum, who was always keen to listen. My enthusiasm never waned, and I coped with everything thrown my way – time passed swiftly as I learned with an energy and drive which helped me to achieve the goals I'd set for myself. However, the time dragged for my mother, and although always ready to encourage and praise my every accomplishment, I knew she was hiding how much my presence was missed at home.

Four years of challenging but rewarding work culminated in a graduation ceremony, an emotional experience for myself and my mother, who watched the presentation bursting with pride. A meal in Leicester city centre rounded off a perfect day, and we returned home to spend a few days together before I took up a new post as a fully-fledged nurse. It was also convenient for my mother to meet her future son-in-law.

A young doctor called Ben Amos had captured my heart and figured significantly in our recent conversations. As he couldn't attend the graduation ceremony, it was arranged for Ben to travel to Castleford the following day to stay with us in our home.

Mum and I were both on an emotional high, firstly due to the graduation ceremony, then the prospect of Ben joining us topped off with the anticipation of my new job. It was a position as a Macmillan nurse based at Castleford, Normanton and District Hospital, a role I knew would prove harrowing but one I anticipated with enthusiasm. During the comprehensive medical training, some of the times I was involved in palliative care reduced me to tears, but never once did I waver in maintaining this as my goal. Naturally, it wasn't easy to witness patients coming to the end of their lives, but it was my privilege to help them maintain their dignity and manage their pain. It remained a continual challenge to separate professional and personal life and still is a constant learning curve of how to box the tragic situations which were an everyday occurrence. On the plus side, working in Castleford would enable me to live at home again, which suited my mother and me. It was also an opportunity to contribute financially to my keep, so it was perfect all around.

Ben arrived and within the first hour claimed my mother's heart. A tad over six feet tall, with fair hair and dreamy blue eyes, which seemed to be constantly laughing, Ben soon convinced my mum he was the one to make me happy and everything was going to work out fine, which was just as well as we'd decided to marry the following summer.

FOUR

HELEN

20th August

Megan insisted on driving to the hospital, and I gave her no argument, the truth being that I was losing my confidence to drive in town and was happy to let my daughter take over. Yesterday we spent the afternoon together while Sam was at nursery. We needed to talk, to dig at those unpleasant facts which couldn't be avoided and it wouldn't be easy for either of us. Megan had questions and I knew my answers to some of them would not be well received. Always one to get straight to the point, my daughter asked how long I'd known about the cancer. The truth was, I'd only been certain since seeing Mr Connors three weeks ago, although I'd had my suspicions long before. I explained how ovarian cancer is one of the most difficult to diagnose, as symptoms can be non-specific. At first, I thought the problem was irritable bowel syndrome – not something you wish to share with everyone.

'But you must have had tests to find out what it is. Why didn't you tell me so I could go with you?' Megan was upset and rightly so. Perhaps I should have told her, but you never stop being a mother and protecting your children from the hard knocks of life. So now I told her of the symptoms and the referral to the consultant, the laparotomy and subsequent diagnosis.

'Could the laparotomy be wrong?' she asked. 'Are there other tests they can do?'

Shaking my head, I tried to look for something positive in all of this but sadly failed. 'It was a pretty thorough procedure done under general anaesthetic. They'd initially tried non-invasive tests, blood tests, and an ultrasound scan. The laparotomy is pretty conclusive, and from what I remember, Mr Connors said the cancer is classed as aggressive and has spread to other areas of the abdomen.' I spoke almost apologetically, knowing how much this was hurting my daughter, my misery pushed from my mind by concern for Megan.

The sterile, ultra-bright waiting area was silent as we took our seats. Not too many patients today, and most of them accompanied, as was I. We sat in a row facing a fish tank and watched tiny colourful fish swimming back and forth; could this feature be an effort to calm our nerves and offset the clinical atmosphere?

I couldn't answer all of Megan's questions, and as we waited, I knew she was quietly compiling a mental list of things to ask, which was fine by me. Perhaps she'd absorb more of the jargon than I had done previously. Perhaps that makes it sound as if Mr Connors was talking down to me, which was in no way accurate. He is a genuine, compassionate man, I'm sure. Admittedly, the shock of the biopsy results hit me harder than I expected. Thinking I was prepared for the worst, it still came as a blow to hear the words, however kindly they were spoken. Maybe Megan should have been with me on that occasion too.

Looking around, I could read signs of agitation in some patients' faces and resignation in others. We all had one thing in common, cancer. Some would recover whilst others would not and I knew to which category I belonged. Somewhere in my mind, I felt the urge to smile at these fellow sufferers, to perhaps begin a community sing-song, which of course I wouldn't – the very thought was ridiculous. I think I was reminded of the stories my grandmother told me about being in the air-raid shelters during the war, fate being as uncertain then as for my fellow patients today. There was only one shelter for the whole street, but despite being packed in like sardines, Gran described how they cheered each other up by singing some of the rousing patriotic songs of the era. Each of the women in the shelter had a husband, son or brother fighting for their freedom, and they were not going to sit at home, moping. They fought too, albeit on a different front line, and by refusing to curtail their day-to-day activities, they contributed in some small way to the war effort. Perhaps I could learn something from my grandmother's attitude to help me through this unexpected dark time.

My turn came after a wait of only twenty minutes and we were ushered in to see Mr Connors. He stood politely to shake hands with Megan and me, obviously pleased I was not alone on this occasion. My daughter seemed the more tense of the two of us, and my concern was focused on her. I'd had longer to contemplate my illness and wrestle with its implications; Megan was still in the first stage of shock. The file with my name lay open on the consultant's desk, but he spoke without the need to refer to it.

'Helen, I'm sure you've thought of things to ask since your last visit, but perhaps you'd like me to go over the biopsy results again so your daughter can hear too?' Wise man – he knew I'd absorbed very few of his words last time and now kindly phrased this offer to save my embarrassment. I nodded and willed myself to concentrate, although my thoughts were of Megan. We sat rather stiffly in the plastic bucket chairs opposite the consultant as he explained again.

GILLIAN JACKSON

'The laparotomy allowed us to examine your ovaries and other organs nearby, and we took several tissue samples. But, I'm sorry to say the cancer has spread from the ovaries to other organs in the pelvic and abdominal area and is what we term 'high grade', a grade-three-type cancer which unfortunately grows more rapidly than most.'

As he paused, I glanced at Megan, whose eyes were filling with tears. The reality of the situation was reflected in the stiffness of her body. Her beautiful, young face was pale and drawn, with tension evident from her profile. I found it hard to believe that this man was talking about my body; surely this wasn't happening to me?

'I'm happy to answer any of your questions.' Mr Connors' voice was soft and encouraging. Megan was first to ask; I had forgotten everything I'd been thinking about since my last appointment.

'Can you remove the cancerous cells? Isn't there an operation you could do?'

'We can operate, but the laparotomy showed several affected areas, and we felt it was better to discuss the options with your mother before contemplating such major surgery.'

'Will an operation get rid of the cancer?' Finally, I'd found my voice.

'Because of the stage of the cancerous cells, operating may not be the right course of action. However, there are other treatments to relieve the symptoms which perhaps you'd like to explore.'

'Are you saying you won't operate?' Megan's voice was barely a whisper. Mr Connors looked sad.

'I'm saying that at this stage, the cancer is too widespread for an operation to be successful and such invasive surgery would probably bring a lot of pain and discomfort without a positive outcome.' The consultant's gaze moved from Megan to me.

'So the cancer isn't going to go away. There's no treatment?' I asked the question which I knew was on Megan's mind.

'That's right, Helen. I'm so sorry. But there are other things we can offer. Chemotherapy could help arrest the spread of cancerous cells, and drugs can help control the symptoms. I suggest you take time to discuss this with your family, and then, if you like, we can arrange an appointment with a Macmillan nurse. There are leaflets here which will give you an idea of the help available, and when you've had time to think it through, we'll see you again.'

We left the doctor's office clutching a wad of leaflets. Megan linked her arm through mine, and we propped each other up on our way back to the car. The sun's warmth didn't seem to reach my body, this body which was betraying me, which was causing physical and emotional pain, this body which was ready to give up its tenuous hold on life. But was I prepared to give up, too? Would there be enough strength or time left to accomplish what I still needed to do?

I suggested to Megan that we call in somewhere for a coffee before returning home to give us a chance to discuss what we'd just been told. She nodded silently, started the engine and headed towards the town centre, but within a couple of minutes, she pulled into the side of the road and switched the engine off. I reached for her hand as she released the flood of tears building up. We held each other as we both cried.

'Let's go home,' I eventually suggested. Megan nodded.

'Mine or yours?' she asked.

'I have chocolate.' I grinned at my daughter.

'Yours it is then!'

The tears were spent, cathartic tears which needed to be shed before we could start the serious business of making decisions. Peppermint tea and dark chocolate were soon by our sides as we sat in the conservatory, the doors wide open, allowing the warmth and light of the sun to access the cold darkness of our thoughts, neither of us wanting to open up the dialogue. Finally, after a brief silence, I decided to come clean on what I was thinking.

'I don't want any treatment, Megan.'

My daughter looked horrified. 'But they can give you chemotherapy... it could – would – give you more time!'

'You heard Mr Connors, the cancer is widespread, and it will win in the end. I don't want to go down that road. From what I've read, the side effects of the treatment are worse than the disease itself. If there was a chance of chemo getting rid of the cancer, it would be different, but anything they offer isn't going to cure me. I'd rather see how I get along without treatment and when the pain gets too much, take medication, which can be tailored to suit my needs.'

'Please, Mum, just think about it.'

'I've thought about nothing else for weeks now, love. I've done a bit of research on the internet, and to have the treatment wouldn't guarantee any extra time. I don't want to live my last days in a permanently nauseous state or lose my hair and all the other side effects it brings. At the moment, it's quite manageable, and quality of life is more important to me than trying to extend it by a few weeks.'

My words sounded harsh, but it was for the best, and I hope Megan will eventually realise I was right. She didn't push too hard to change my mind, and the conversation thankfully turned to the plans I'd made for the immediate future – the only kind of future I have left – to visit Luke in Canada.

As I hugged Megan before she left for home, my daughter struggled to compose herself, trying so hard to be brave. Incidents from her childhood came to mind, other times when she'd tried to be so grown up, a big girl and not a baby. I recalled images of her first day at school as she followed the other children into the classroom with her tiny fists clenched at her sides, biting her bottom lip to stop the tears from falling. Visits to the dentist and the time she fell out with her best friend popped into my head, and I squeezed my daughter harder, love for her welling up inside until I thought I'd burst. As we parted I turned to Gus. A long walk with my dog was precisely what I needed to bring perspective to my muddled mind. I still had much for which to be grateful.

FIVE

HELEN

21st August

This morning I reluctantly kept an appointment with my GP, who'd already heard from Mr Connors and was up to date on my current health issues. His room was warm and rather airless, although the window was open. It was a muggy day, hot and still without as much as a hint of a breeze to make the heat more bearable and Dr Dean was, unusually, in his shirtsleeves. I told him of my decision not to have chemotherapy, which hardly surprised him. We discussed how best to proceed, and I requested a referral to a Macmillan nurse, which he was happy to endorse as the best way forward. Dr Dean then inquired about my general health and what problems the cancer was giving me so far. I took the opportunity to tell him of my plans to travel to Canada, asking his opinion. As expected, he advised me to go as soon as possible and offered to write a letter to my travel insurers saying I was still fit to travel. I hadn't thought about insurance, so accepted the offer hoping it would satisfy any issues raised. Once back at home, I spent the rest of the morning on my laptop, booking the first available flight to Canada on the second of September.

Before leaving the country, I felt it prudent to visit my solicitor, not that I expected to die in Canada, but well, you know. An appointment was made, and a week before my trip, I found myself in John Palmer's dusty office, reviewing my will. There were not many changes to be made; after Andrew died, the will was updated, and the house was put in trust for Megan and Luke, but I wanted to know everything was in order. John had been Andrew's friend and handled all our legal affairs since we were married. He and Andrew played golf together, and I'd become friendly with his wife, Margaret, whom I occasionally met for coffee. It was a pretty straightforward will – everything to be divided equally between Luke and Megan, with John acting as executor. I had a list of bequests I wanted to include, gifts to a small number of charities and a few personal items to close friends. John offered to make the amendments that day and send a copy in the post for me to sign in front of witnesses and return to him before I left for Canada.

2nd September

Incredible! I'm sitting on the aircraft – the beginning of my big adventure – trying to catch up with the journal. The last few days have been so busy preparing for this trip and spending time with Megan and Sam that my writing has been sadly neglected. Consciously trying to breathe steadily, I focus on the holiday side of my trip rather than the reason for it. Seeing Luke again and finally meeting my youngest grandson will be wonderful.

Despite frequent reassurances to Megan to the contrary, I felt more than a little apprehensive about travelling alone. On all previous holidays I'd tagged along behind Andrew, trusting he knew everything we needed to do to arrive safely at our destination. My son-in-law, James, drove me to the station, where I was to catch a train to London. He and Megan had insisted I use a private hire car to meet me at King's Cross and drive to Heathrow. The alternative was to find a taxi to Paddington station and catch the train to Heathrow. The hire car option proved much more straightforward, yet it felt strange seeing the driver on the platform holding up a sign which read, '*Ms Reid*'. Terry, the driver, was friendly and efficient, effortlessly stowing my luggage in the car boot and driving competently through the busy city to drop me in good time at Heathrow's terminal two. Finding the correct check-in desk brought instant relief as my luggage disappeared on the conveyor belt. But standing alone in the vast, busy lobby, watching the flight information scroll down the board above my head, was suddenly confusing and more than a little daunting. Each time I identified my flight number on the list, it disappeared, and I stood for what seemed like ages, waiting for it to come around again. Feeling rather foolish, I glanced from my boarding pass to the list several times until satisfied I'd correctly identified the flight departure gate and when I needed to be there.

It's the first time I've flown from Heathrow, a much larger airport than I'd imagined, and I found the place somewhat daunting. Previous trips abroad have been from either Newcastle or Manchester, which could fit together into the almost five-square-mile site Heathrow occupies. Fortunately, it's well signposted, and after walking for nearly twenty minutes, using the welcome moving walkways, I arrived at the gate two hours before take-off time.

Being early is inbred into my DNA, or so Andrew always told me. He was much more laid back about time, leaving me to worry about being late. I suppose we complemented each other in that respect and usually managed to arrive at events, or places, in a reasonable time. Being in an unfamiliar place is much more challenging when alone. With Andrew, our trip began at the airport, where we'd relax with coffee after checking in the luggage and watch the world go by. However, the airport seemed somewhat intimidating on my own, and I found myself seeking a quiet corner where I could take my Starbucks coffee and hopefully blend into the vast waiting area, which was gate number 67.

It's easy to understand why people feel lonely in a crowd. As I watched the continuous stream of passing family groups and couples, a degree of envy settled heavily on my heart. I needed to remind myself that I've had my share of the carefree, happy family life evident all around me, and still do. I have two happy, healthy children and two gorgeous grandchildren, much more than many people ever have. However, it's all relative, and I refuse to think of what I no longer have and steer my thoughts to the positive. After all, I was on my way to meet Ethan and spend time with Luke and Imogen. I need to enjoy every precious minute with them and leave the future to worry about itself.

The seating inside the plane was different from any I'd encountered before, configured with two aisles between three blocks of seating. It was somewhat disconcerting to think I would be seated next to a stranger for over nine hours during this journey. But at least my seat was next to the window, so if I dozed off, I'd have something to lean on other than a stranger's shoulder. The downside is that to get out of my seat, I would need to disturb two other passengers.

I was the first to be seated in row F and settled down quickly, with my hand luggage pushed under the seat in front, a magazine, my journal and a couple of boiled sweets to suck during take-off. My heart pounded rapidly as a buzz of excitement filled the plane, children laughed and played, and generally, there was a positive atmosphere, which didn't quite seem to reach me, although I was also a traveller.

A tall man, perhaps in his early sixties, sat in the seat next to mine, smiling politely as he struggled to fold his long legs into the inadequate allotted space. Returning his smile, I buried my head into the journal as he eventually found a comfortable position. His hand luggage consisted of one well-worn leather briefcase, which he squeezed under the seat in front. After a few minutes, the cabin crew began their routine safety announcements as we taxied down the runway. My adventure was underway. I dutifully put my journal away to pay attention to the cabin crew.

3rd September

A wall of heat engulfed me as I stepped from the plane. It felt almost tangible, as if I could push it away from my weary body, which of course, I couldn't, and I made my way into the arrivals lounge, carried along with the other passengers who'd been on the same flight. Within an hour, which dragged as I waited for my luggage on the slow-moving carousel, I was in the arms of my handsome six-foot-five son, who was waiting to lift me off my feet, crushing my stiff body into his, with both of us laughing and crying simultaneously. Such an emotional reunion took me by surprise, and as Luke grabbed my luggage in one effortless move, he steered me to the airport exit. Keen as I was to meet Ethan, I was delighted to have Luke to myself for the journey to his home, and as he did most of the talking, I relaxed and enjoyed the sound of his voice and his comfortable, familiar presence. His chatter was happy, almost childlike, and it was so good to see him. The time for my news could wait. I was weary and needed rest; my body clock was confused with sleep long overdue; there'd been very little during the flight.

When I arrived at Luke and Imogen's house, my daughter-in-law greeted me warmly and placed a mug of tea in my hand almost as soon as I walked through the door. Unfortunately, Ethan was in bed, so meeting him would have to wait until the next day. Imogen showed me to my room, seeming to understand my need to rest, and within an hour, the house was quiet, with all its occupants soundly asleep.

As so often happens these days, my sleep was broken after only three hours by a desperate need to go to the bathroom, after which I was suddenly wide awake. So here I am again, recording the events of the past twenty-four hours in my journal – and the bittersweet emotions awakened by meeting fellow traveller, Tim.

I couldn't have anticipated what happened on the flight. Having put away my journal to concentrate on the safety demonstration, I settled back in the seat, watching through the window as the plane began to move. There was a knot in my stomach as the plane stopped, and the engine roared loudly before accelerating and leaving the tarmac. It was a smooth, if noisy, take-off, and as the plane swiftly put distance between us and the ground below, I studied the clusters of houses, the fields and trees until they were too small to see anymore, and a blanket of cloud separated the earth from our plane. Turning away from the window, I again became aware of the man beside me who smiled and offered his hand.

'It seems we're to spend the next several hours together; my name's Tim.' The inflexion at the end of the sentence implied he expected an answer, so I shook his hand and, returning the smile, told him my name. A few polite questions followed as we discussed our destination and where we would travel after landing in Vancouver. When the service trolley came around,

Tim insisted on buying me a coffee, and our conversation continued as we quickly grew comfortable in each other's company. I told him I was visiting my son and travelling alone because my husband had died before we could make the trip together. It hardly seemed appropriate to tell a virtual stranger I was carrying the news of my impending death to my son. Tim was also widowed and had been for twelve years, during which time he admitted to having struggled with life alone. I assumed he referred to an emotional struggle, something with which I could readily identify. I learned that Tim held a responsible position as the director of an international software company. His slight Scottish accent and soft voice made him easy to listen to and I became engrossed in the anecdotes he related with gentle, good-natured humour.

Tim was undeniably attractive, and I couldn't help but wonder why he hadn't remarried; surely, plenty of single women would have considered him a good catch. I mentally scolded myself for being so nosey – I've always loved a good romance and am a sucker for a happy ending, yet now I was learning the hard way how real life didn't always end happily ever after. Still, I wanted to know more about this man, to listen to his stories and watch how his whole face lit up when he smiled. Okay, perhaps I was acting like a schoolgirl with a crush, but I was experiencing feelings I'd never expected to have again.

I have to admit to being attracted to Tim. Only two hours into a flight which would take at least another seven, I was sitting next to a handsome man and inwardly acknowledged I wanted to get to know him better. Feeling the need to stretch my legs, I squeezed past Tim and the young man on his other side, who appeared to be permanently glued to a tablet screen, and set off to walk up and down the aisle as far as possible and pay a visit to the bathroom.

Away from Tim's proximity, I could think straight. It was a

situation which could never develop into anything other than a fleeting encounter. We were simply filling in time before reaching our destination – at my age and in my situation, anything more was impossible. Returning to my seat, another coffee waited for me, reminding me how it was these little kindnesses which I'd missed so much since Andrew died – someone holding the car door open, making tea or coffee when I was tired, and the comfort of another's physical presence. After three years without my husband, I was still coming to terms with his loss, although now aware there were not many months left for me to mourn.

Thanking Tim, I insisted it was my turn to pay next time and once again we fell into easy conversation. He told me of his two daughters, both grown up, like my children and very dear to him. I asked polite questions and learned he had one grandchild, a seven-year-old boy and hoped for more in the future. I told him about Sam and Ethan, whom I was shortly to meet.

Another hour passed as we talked. Outside grew dark, and many passengers were asleep, including 'tablet man' on Tim's other side. My body felt tired, but I didn't want to waste precious time sleeping, knowing I'd never see this lovely man again after this flight. I stifled a yawn. Tim cupped his hand over mine and gently squeezed. I almost jumped at the physical contact, which simultaneously felt alien yet so right and comforting.

'You must be tired and I've been selfish in monopolising you. Shall I ask the stewardess for a blanket for you?' His eyes expressed genuine concern, and I found my own filling with tears.

'What's wrong, Helen? Is it something I've said?' Tim was anxious. I shook my head and attempted a smile.

'No, not at all. Perhaps I am tired.'

Attracting the attention of a stewardess, he asked for a blanket. She came back quickly with a blanket and a small pillow, both sealed in plastic covers. I thanked her before unwrapping them and trying to get comfortable enough to sleep. Tim, too, put his head back and closed his eyes, for which I was grateful.

I was experiencing a whole gamut of emotions which seemed to be almost tearing me apart from the inside. What is it the psychologists call it? PLOM, the 'Poor Little Old Me' syndrome? For the first time since cancer had been diagnosed, I was angry. Why did this have to happen to me, hadn't I suffered enough? I had no doubt it was my travelling companion who prompted these feelings and, having never expected to meet anyone to whom I would be the least attracted, I was both shocked and bemused. After Andrew died, the thought of another man's closeness was almost abhorrent. He'd been the great love of my life, no one could ever mean as much to me, and I couldn't imagine anyone ever taking his place. The thought of physical closeness with anyone else almost repelled me, but that was before I met Tim. Now I had to admit I was fantasising about a physical relationship with this man, whom I'd met only two or three hours ago! Shame on me. I kept my eyes firmly closed for fear they would betray the inappropriate thoughts dancing through my mind.

After a while, I became aware of Tim's slow and steady breathing, indicating he, at least, was managing to sleep. I opened my eyes and turned to look at his profile. His features were strong and well-proportioned, eyelids hiding the soft brown eyes I'd already admired and long lashes resting on his cheeks. His skin was lightly tanned and unblemished, and his hair curled attractively over his collar, soft and golden, streaked with grey, which added to the attraction rather than marring his appearance.

As I watched Tim sleep, I indulged my thoughts and travelled to the world of *what if*. If I didn't have cancer this could be the prelude to a romantic liaison. If we'd met even a year ago, perhaps we could have found happiness in each other's company. If I knew how much longer I had to live, maybe we could offer comfort and companionship to each other, albeit temporarily. But it was a stupid game thinking such things, and in my heart, I knew it to be so. Yet this stranger had taken me by surprise, or rather my feelings for this stranger had taken me by surprise. The reality was there was no future in pursuing any kind of relationship, platonic or otherwise, and it would be utterly unfair to Tim to do so. The question was, should I tell him the truth? Not such an easy question. If I told him, it might elicit sympathy or pity, neither of which I wanted, and what would be the point anyway? It would be best to keep things light and pleasant and enjoy each other's company for the duration of the flight, which was possibly all he wanted anyway.

The anger interplayed with bitterness in my mind and possibly marked the moment when I realised precisely what was happening to my body and how utterly final the diagnosis was. It was an epiphany. I was going to die, and there was nothing anyone could do about it. The realisation that dying meant there was no longer a future to live for and plan suddenly struck me. Previously I thought only of the next few months and how to cope whilst making the most of the time. Now I began to ponder the finality of death. Was it simply an ending, coming up against a brick wall? Or was it a doorway, a portal into some kind of afterlife? Never having thought deeply about such issues before, it seemed too much to comprehend now. I was reminded of what someone once told me about being blind; to understand blindness, closing your eyes is no good – you can still see darkness, an inky black. Try looking into the inside of your shoe with your big toe – that comes nearer the mark. But can this kind of analogy apply to death?

Quite simply, I did not have a future to plan for or dream about. Death was approaching whether I understood it, wanted it, or not. If only I could rip the cancer out of my body – but it was too far on to do so. Tears escaped and trickled down my cheeks, blurring the sight of the sleeping man beside me. Meeting Tim had somehow urged me to want to fight this cancer, but I knew it had already won the battle, and all I could do was control the pain it brought and make the time left count for something. The tyranny of *what if* was cruelly racing through my mind. I needed to banish it entirely, to live in the moment.

So, you are probably wondering what became of Tim. Before we landed in Canada, he asked if we could keep in touch (I'd have been disappointed if he hadn't) but there was no point in doing so. Without giving the real reason, I fudged an answer about it being the wrong time for me, which was perfectly true. In another life, I would almost certainly have agreed and readily moved on with a relationship, at least to see where it took us. Yet meeting Tim only served to reinforce the finality of my life, and I didn't tell you then as it was one more road I knew I could never travel and an episode which left me more than a little sad. I shall try to sleep now and concentrate on tomorrow rather than yesterday.

SIX
HELEN

4th September

I was completely lost with time. Waking in an unfamiliar room, confusion blurred my thinking for a moment or two until the previous day flooded back into my mind. It was daytime, the sun high in the sky and the sound of subdued chatter coming from below. I pulled a robe over my nightdress and set off to find my family. Following the sound led me to the kitchen, where Luke and Imogen were seated at the table while their excited little boy played with cars on the floor. He jumped up when he saw me and ran to his mother's side.

'Ethan! You've been pestering to meet Grandma all morning, and now she's here, you pretend to be shy!' Imogen hugged her son and Luke jumped up to kiss me and put the kettle on. Although I'd seen Ethan many times on Skype, it was only now that I could see the resemblance to his father; the child was so like Luke had been at the same age – it prompted memories which flitted through my mind like an old reel of film. Sitting at the table beside Imogen, I decided to wait until Ethan came to me rather than attempt to draw him out. I smiled and said good morning to my grandson before turning my attention to his parents.

'Are you not going to work today, Luke?'

'Not on your first day here, Mum. I have the whole week off in honour of your visit!'

I was delighted and accepted the tea he offered. Ethan moved away from his mother and picked up the cars from the floor. He brought one over to me and pushed it back and forth on the table.

'I like your car. Is it the one you showed me last week when we spoke?'

Ethan smiled, recognition in his eyes. 'Are you my grandma?'

'I certainly am, and you're my grandson! I've waited a long time to meet you.' Ethan was suddenly on my knee, running the car up my arm and over my head. I squeezed his thin little body and he laughed, wriggling down to the floor again. Gaining Ethan's trust was the easy part of this trip. Breaking the news to Luke and Imogen would be much more challenging.

Yesterday's journey had taken its toll on my body, most acutely in my lower back, an unwelcome, familiar sensation. I needed my medication but would wait until after breakfast.

'I thought we'd stay close to home today, perhaps go out for a walk if you're up to it so you can see where we live. It's a great little community.' Luke was grinning like a child on Christmas morning, and I was touched when my presence so obviously pleased him. Nodding in agreement, I nibbled at a slice of toast.

'Don't you want pancakes, Grandma?' Ethan frowned.

'Toast's just fine for me, Ethan, thank you.'

'Well, can I have your pancakes?'

I laughed at the ulterior motive as his mother limited him to just one more. He'd already eaten three.

After breakfast, I returned to my room to unpack, but first, find my medication to take the much-needed dose and then hide it on the top of the wardrobe where I could reach, but Ethan couldn't. Gazing from the window, I could see what a beautiful place Luke had chosen to live. Travelling beside him from Vancouver International Airport, my focus had been almost solely on him and I barely registered the stunning views around us. I lost track of how long the journey took, but I remember the ferry crossing from the aptly named Horseshoe Bay Ferry Terminal and the forty minutes or so until we reached Langdale Ferry Terminal. Gibsons Landing, our destination, was only ten minutes from there. The eventful journey was over, and a full day stretched before me to spend with Luke, Imogen and Ethan.

The view from the bedroom window was picture postcard material, the Pacific Ocean shimmering gloriously in the morning sunlight and only a few tempting yards away from the house. I dressed quickly, suddenly anxious to be outside and exploring my son's new world. The serious talking could wait until the evening. We'd enjoy at least one carefree day together.

'We'll not go too far today, Mum; you must be tired. I thought we'd leave the car and walk around Gibsons Landing and up to Gibson itself.' It sounded perfect, a chance to stretch my limbs after sitting for all those hours on the aircraft. As we set off, Ethan overcame all previous shyness to hold my hand, appointing himself an official tour guide and proudly boasting how he would show me everything. The weather was faultless, not too hot but pleasant enough to discard the layers of clothes I'd packed, unsure of what would be needed. Firstly, we circled the perimeter of the house. Like the other nearby dwellings, it was a pretty clapboard house on three levels. The lower floor opened onto a veranda with a stony path leading directly to the Pacific Ocean.

'We can throw stones into the sea if you like, Grandma?' Ethan grinned, waiting for my approval.

'I'd love to! Maybe when we come back from our walk?' The deal was sealed, with my grandson putting his warm little hand into mine as he happily led the way. We circumvented the house to walk toward Gibson, and the pleasant surroundings struck me. Almost every home was individually designed and painted in soft pastels or warm terracotta. With the sun shining and the air heavily scented with salt from the ocean, it felt like walking through the set of an episode of *Murder, She Wrote*. Hopefully, there'd be no murders to complicate this easy-going, relaxed little place. We passed a few shops selling upmarket ladies' clothes and designer home accessories and stopped at each one to peer into the attractive windows before moving on to the next.

Near the marina overlooking the harbour was a delightful bar and restaurant called Molly's Reach where we stopped for coffee and entered the wonderfully sleepy atmosphere. Ethan ordered a milkshake, which was almost as big as he was, but Imogen assured me he'd be equal to it, and he was. We chose coffee and a slice of blueberry pie; I could get used to this kind of life. Refreshed, we moved on a little further, and the road began to climb, affording an amazing view of the 'sunshine coast'. When we eventually turned to head back to Gibsons Landing, I was made to feel quite at home by the sight of Mike's Plaice, a traditional fish and chip shop. Luke seemed to sense when I was growing weary and suggested lunch at home and rest before deciding to do anything else. I readily agreed – although it was good to see my son's adopted hometown, where he and Imogen were happily settled, and Ethan knew no other.

I retired to my room for an hour after lunch, promising Ethan that we could skim stones into the ocean when I awoke. Sleep came immediately. Perhaps the jet lag was catching up, and when I eventually woke, it was to the sound of tapping on the bedroom door. Ethan came in, dressed in swimming trunks and slathered in sun cream. It was time to fulfil my promise, and the next hour was happily spent skimming stones and delighting in Ethan's squeals of delight when his stones reached further than mine. Luke came out to join us whilst Imogen busied herself in the kitchen.

'It's so good to have you here, Mum. I'm only sorry Dad never made the trip out here to see where we settled.' Luke stood beside me, his arm protectively around my shoulders and I leaned into him, trying to draw some of his strength and vitality into my tired body. In such a charming setting, anyone could be forgiven for thinking how good life was, and I felt a stab of guilt knowing I was soon about to spoil the perfection of Luke's life, that this moment was fleeting and would very soon be lost to us all.

Later in the evening, when Ethan was in bed, I knew the time was right to tell Luke why I'd come. It seemed almost cruel to deflate the holiday atmosphere, but leaving the news until my visit's end would undoubtedly be more hurtful. They'd need time to accept and process this news and I wanted to be with them as they did.

The three of us sat on the veranda, enjoying the last of the day's sunshine and the cool breeze rippling across the water. It seemed a sin to spoil such a perfect moment, but it needed to be done, even though I struggled to find the right words.

'I've been having some health problems lately...' My throat was suddenly dry. Luke's eyes swivelled towards me as I tried to continue.

'I've seen a specialist at the hospital... and it seems I have ovarian cancer.' Unfortunately, there was no way to dress it up – to ease the pain such news inevitably brought. Luke's face fell, as did Imogen's, making me feel like the killjoy who spoiled the party.

'But it can be cured, can't it?'

'No, Luke, it's spread too far. There's nothing the doctor can do except prescribe medication for the pain, which will worsen at the end.'

'What about chemotherapy or an operation? Surely they can try something?'

'It's too late for surgery, and chemotherapy won't cure the cancer, and at best, would only give me a few more weeks, or a month or two, so I've decided not to go down that route. Chemotherapy will undoubtedly have worse side effects than letting the cancer take its course, so I'd prefer to enjoy my last few months rather than struggle with the effects of chemotherapy.'

Luke moved to sit beside me on the sofa, his arm around my shoulder. Relaxing into his strong body, I allowed my silent tears to flow, as did my son. We stayed silent for several minutes, the only sound being the waves gently lapping onto the stones. Luke would have more questions in the coming days, but for now, his presence brought me comfort as I hope mine did for him. Imogen tiptoed into the house, returning soon with tea, her eyes red and puffy. As she poured the tea, I caught her hand and squeezed it, grateful for her silent support of me and Luke. We would talk again and hopefully enjoy our days together, even knowing they were numbered. Ethan was around to keep our spirits high, he was the future, and I was so glad to have this time to get to know him, to be a grandma even for such a short time, and shower him with my love.

SEVEN

HELEN

2 1st September

Canada seems just a distant memory now. The parting was so hard, with tears, hugs and promises from us all. Leaving Ethan, I held his tiny frame in my arms, whispering how much I loved him and hoping he would remember me in years to come. Luke plans to come home and visit before too long, which makes sense because we both know I don't have much time. His promise was comforting; perhaps I will see him again before I die.

My homeward journey was uneventful. A small part of me was hoping Tim would be on the same flight, but I hadn't seen him and knew it was pointless wishing for something which could never be. Meeting him had given me a tantalising insight into what the future could have been, but the cancer growing within my body colours my future and reminds me of the stark reality of having only a short measure of time left. There will be no romance with Tim or anyone else; I simply do not have a future.

A couple of lazy days were in order on my return home, catching up with Megan, James and Sam, whose excitement at seeing me again is a balm to my weary body and soul. Visiting my mother was also high on the priority list, so I set off to the residential home where she lived the second morning after my return. While I was in Canada, Megan had visited a couple of times, visits which Mum no doubt would not remember.

Entering the home, I signed in and went to the dayroom, a room which could easily be found by following the noise of the television, always loud but never quite loud enough for many of the residents. There were other quieter rooms to use, but the television appeared to draw them to it, even though no one seemed to be watching the usual fodder of daytime programmes.

Mum was in the far corner, slumped in a wheelchair, her mouth moving as if in conversation but with no discernible words being formed. She barely looked at me yet didn't protest as I wheeled her from the dayroom along the passage to her bedroom. The matron passed us and asked if I would stop by her office on the way out, to which I agreed. Her request was nothing unusual and I presumed it would be to update me of any changes in medication or other such detail. Mum's room was relatively spacious and clean and boasted a tiny bathroom and television, which was probably a waste now, it was so rarely switched on. Lapsing into the usual one-sided conversation, I chatted about my visit to see Luke and Imogen and told her all about her great-grandson. It didn't appear to register, but this was the norm and I continued to fill the void in the room with words.

When Mum dozed off, I took the opportunity to tidy her clothes and see if she needed anything. It amazed me how shabby the clothes looked after only a relatively short time, probably due to being laundered daily. Even the blouse she was wearing, which I have no doubt was clean this morning, had tea stains and something I suspected to be marmalade down the front. Perhaps I should make a list and ensure she had everything she needed before I...

I'm doing this a lot lately, calmly thinking I must do something and mentally adding, 'before I die'. Does this mean I've accepted it or simply that I'm a control and list freak? Whatever, it was another thing I could do to ease the burden on Megan – for afterwards. Mum was chattering in her sleep, something Andrew always said I did too, words which made no sense, the consequence of medication, no doubt. I began tidying the top of the drawers and, opening a trinket box to put a watch away, found a small cache of gold and silver jewellery which I didn't recognise as Mum's. Puzzled, I knew she wouldn't be able to explain them, so leaving them where they were, I thought I'd mention it to the matron later.

Mum woke with a start and began shouting something about fighting. Trying to calm her only made her cries even louder, so I rang the bell for help. A nurse came almost immediately; she'd been on her way with a cup of tea which she set on the table and began to try and calm Mum down. However, she would not be pacified and in a fit of throwing her arms around she knocked the table over, sending the tea across the carpet and the cup shattering into pieces. Another nurse appeared with a sedative which seemed to calm her down relatively quickly, and as they cleared up the mess, Mum sat smiling at us all as if nothing had happened. This was not like my mother at all. True, she mostly talked nonsense these days and often sang at inappropriate times, but she was generally a sweet old lady, oblivious to life being played out around her. Mum had lost her memories of those close to her and occasionally asked me who I was or who I'd come to visit. It was sad, but this angry outburst was something new. Eventually, when it was clear Mum needed to sleep, I kissed her goodbye and left the room, going in search of the matron. She was in her office and asked me to sit down.

'Your mother's had a few issues lately. I knew you were away and didn't want to trouble your daughter, but she seems to be having episodes of rather violent behaviour for no apparent reason.' Her words were a shock; my mother was a tiny, birdlike lady who'd grown increasingly frail during the last couple of years, but today I'd witnessed it for myself. Neither of us could think of anything which might have brought this on; it's not uncommon for people living with Alzheimer's to be violent, but it was concerning for it to come on suddenly. I asked if her doctor had visited, to which the matron said the doctor on call had prescribed sedatives, but she would call Mum's GP if I preferred, and I could be there when he came. Satisfied with this, I was about to leave when I remembered the jewellery. The matron seemed puzzled too, so we returned to Mum's room and I showed her the items which did not belong there. She agreed to take them to her office and enquire if other residents were missing any items. I finally left, wondering what had changed my mother into a somewhat violent old lady with magpie tendencies.

Once home, I found a message from a Macmillan nurse asking me to ring and arrange a meeting. My GP had set the wheels in motion and I was keen to find out what kind of help was available. When I managed to get through to the right person, a lady called Rachel Amos, we arranged a time to meet. She was happy to visit me at home, which was my preference, too; I think I shall see more than enough of hospitals and clinics during the next few months.

Rachel is a tall, graceful lady with beautiful curly red hair, worn shoulder-length, a mass of freckles and a wide attractive smile. There are times when you know instantly you will connect with another person, and this was one of those moments for me. We hit it off immediately, and over coffee in my small conservatory, warmed by the late-morning sun streaming through the window, I asked some of the questions I'd been storing up. Rachel patiently answered, imparting impressive knowledge and experience in a simple, sensitive way, relaxing me and endearing herself to me. She was candid, telling me nothing was taboo, I could ask anything, and if she didn't know the answer, she'd do her best to find out.

Dying is not a straightforward experience, or at least not when you know roughly when the event will occur. I hoped to be around at Christmas and well enough to be independent and still caring for myself. However, predicting what the new year and next spring would hold was impossible. Rachel talked me through some of the options I might like to consider, namely the hospice, of which she couldn't speak highly enough, and the drugs available as the pain increased. It's been well over a month since the cancer was confirmed, and I was coping reasonably well – regarding pain, anyway. If anything, I was probably putting up with it, trying to be brave, but Rachel asked quite bluntly why I would 'put up with pain' when there was medication to help. It suddenly seemed ridiculous, it wasn't as if I had to worry about the long-term effects of any drugs prescribed for me, so I decided – bring it on! Why not?

In painting an overall picture of what help and support were available, Rachel introduced me to the world of Macmillan cancer support. I learned of a band of volunteers who could offer assistance with practical things, such as shopping or lifts to appointments. In addition, they have experts in financial matters who can help with any needs related to cancer. She also asked if I'd like to visit the hospice, explaining how they offered more than just a comfortable place for the last days, such as support groups and respite care, which must be a relief for those without a family to support them.

I felt blessed knowing my family would be there for me throughout this trial. Megan and James couldn't do enough now, and I was also financially stable, a fortunate position in which to be. It was an excellent first contact and I liked Rachel immensely. She left her office telephone number with me to get in touch and suggested I check out their website, where there were online support groups and people in similar situations to interact with if I wished. It seemed as if everything was covered, and it certainly helped to know I'd not be alone in this strange and unsettling experience.

Rachel left me with much to ponder on the day but visited again later in the week.

'Just popping in to see everything's all right,' she said. It was comforting to know she was there, in the background, to provide any help or answer any questions I might have. However, there are still other pressing things to do, and I no longer have the luxury of wasting my precious time.

EIGHT
RACHEL

On several occasions over the years, friends have questioned my vocation of working in palliative care. I can understand why and appreciate their concern, but strange though it may seem, I rarely find my job 'morbid' or 'depressing', words they see as synonymous with my role in nursing. Very often, it's the antithesis of morbid – I am privileged to meet some remarkable people from whom I learn much about life and death. True, there are patients for whom the end of life is borne in loneliness, and I wish I could do more for them. Not everyone has a supportive family to see them through such a difficult period, and yes, there are occasions when I feel inadequate. But, there are places and people who offer help to those who are alone. I'm an enthusiastic advocate of hospices, having seen their fantastic work and the excellent care they provide. I often direct patients to such facilities, which include far more than simply providing a place to spend their latter days.

Much of my work involves signposting patients to the right place for the right kind of help. This can include the hospice, financial advice or practical support such as shopping or whatever may present problems. From an outsider's point of view, my work must seem gloomy, but I have my own family to come home to, a home filled with such love and happiness that if depression tried to rear its ugly head, it would last no more than a minute! Besides, not all of my patients die and many successfully battle cancer before moving on to lead happy and fulfilled lives. I view it a privilege to meet many courageous people and help them through their difficult days and on to a full recovery.

A cancer diagnosis brings great fear, yet often becomes a time of growth and can unite a couple, or a family, to make them stronger than before. It puts life into perspective, and I've seen such a diagnosis rebuild a marriage, reunite fractured families and bring love and compassion into the lives of those it touches. Humour is a great tool that many of my patients use to get through those tough times. I've laughed with women trying on wigs and have heard all manner of jokes about breasts and boob jobs. I can't pretend it's an easy job, and there've been weeks when I've attended more than one funeral, but even then, there is a celebration in a life well-lived.

My husband, Ben, is totally supportive of all I do. We married twelve months after we graduated. He was more than happy to move to Castleford, so we could be near Mum, who, needless to say, was delighted, not only at her daughter coming home but also to acquire a son-in-law. I owe so much to Mum and can't imagine not being close to her, both geographically and emotionally.

A year after our wedding, we were delighted to learn I was pregnant, and Mum was a big part of that *we*. I took maternity leave, starting just a couple of weeks before Charlotte was born, and although this was the beginning of a new role for me as a mother, there was no doubt I would go back to nursing. Ben and I discussed childcare and looked at various nurseries when we should have known the answer was right on our doorstep.

Admittedly the thought of asking Mum to look after our daughter had occurred to me, but I didn't wish to assume anything or hold any expectations. She'd only recently retired, and we hesitated to broach the subject, but we didn't have to.

'I know you've been looking at nurseries for Charlotte...' Mum said one day, 'but if you'd like... and if you think I'd be suitable, I'd very much like to look after her.'

'Oh, Mum, that would be marvellous. We didn't want you to think we had expectations, and now you're retired, you should be using the time to do what you want. Are you sure about this?'

'Well, this *is* what I want to do! I'm not the sort to join over-sixties clubs and the like. I didn't want to push myself in case you prefer professional childcare.'

Ben jumped in at this point. 'Martha, you've done such a wonderful job with Rachel and I don't think we could find anyone better qualified. I only ask that if it becomes too much for you, you'll tell us, okay?'

It was settled, and Mum was again on hand to help when needed. I have to say I would have floundered without her presence, particularly during those first few weeks after the birth. Mum was a rock. My precious firstborn was a good baby but possessed an absolute novice for a mother. Some of the books I read beforehand told me how motherhood would all come naturally, and once a good routine was established, the baby would thrive and be happy and content. Not in our household!

The first big disappointment was when I couldn't manage to breastfeed, which I'd been determined to do. The midwife and health visitor pushed for me to keep trying when the reality was I felt so inadequate, and me a nurse! It was Mum who eventually sorted it out. I developed abscesses, which were so painful that I had to stop feeding. The health visitor suggested I express the milk, which was also painful. Mum finally took over one afternoon and put me to bed while she bottle-fed my baby. When I eventually stopped berating myself for not being the perfect mother, we settled into a blissfully happy routine. Bottle-feeding was so convenient, and Charlotte could be fed by her daddy, Grandma or me, and if we were all around at the same time, we almost fought for the joy of doing so! Mum was with me every step of the way, her generosity and care made returning to work much easier.

Two years later, I fell pregnant again. We were thrilled, and I was much more relaxed with this pregnancy, determined to enjoy our second time being parents without putting myself under pressure about doing things the right way. Mum wanted to continue looking after Charlotte and the new baby but I was concerned it could prove too much for her. Taking maternity leave allowed me to spend more time with Charlotte and Mum and the strong bond the two had developed was a delight to see. A solution to suit everyone came when we found a nursery for Charlotte three days a week. Our daughter loved other children and company in general, and when we took her to look around a few local nurseries, we had a problem persuading her to leave! Accepting a place each Monday, Wednesday, and Friday suited us all. Ben or I could drop Charlotte at nursery and pick her up whilst Mum would spend time with Katy and both girls on Tuesday and Thursday.

Katy Martha Amos was born in the spring, an appropriate time for new birth. Whereas Charlotte has my red hair and fair, freckled skin, Katy appears to have inherited her father's Nordic looks, with fair hair in soft wisps on the top of her head. I love her newborn smell and the way she screws up her little face as if trying to make sense of this strange new world she's suddenly entered.

Charlotte is fantastic with her new little sister. Arriving

home from the hospital, it was to a house festooned with pink bunting and balloons, the work of my daughter and her grandmother. Being a big sister suits her down to the ground, and she's so helpful and willing, passing nappies or rattling the soft toys to catch Katy's attention. I have everything I could wish for, a wonderful family and a fascinating, fulfilling job in which I can offer comfort to those at the end of their lives. It sometimes scares me how perfect everything is; do I deserve all this?

It's strange how such thoughts intrude on occasions, perhaps due to my work and regularly seeing patients struggling with pain or loneliness. Whatever the reason, living each day to the full is what I aim to do, and helping patients whenever possible is nothing short of a privilege. At times I feel my life is so perfect and it can't last, but then I ask myself why not and determinedly live in the moment. Doing the job I love makes me so thankful for my blessings and determined to help my patients as much as possible.

Much of my working day is spent simply listening. It's essential for patients to be heard and with a hundred per cent attention. Being listened to is a sign of being valued, something we all need to feel. Some patients tell me about their past, wanting me to know what kind of life they've led. Others talk about their families, children, grandchildren, siblings, or whatever's important to them. It's impossible to generalise what each patient wants from our relationship, but I try to meet their needs with the limited contact we have.

Of course, there are those to whom I feel particularly attached; I wouldn't be human if I wasn't touched by the people I meet. One of my recently referred patients seems troubled but hides it so well. Undoubtedly, being diagnosed with cancer is an anxious time, whatever the prognosis, but with Helen Reid, I suspect it goes deeper than simply the illness. On occasions, it seems she wants to tell me something yet cannot bring herself to do so. Generally, our time together goes well; she readily asks questions and understands what is happening to her body, but I can sense an underlying issue which robs her of the peace she craves.

Helen is a very likeable lady, and how she handles the cancer is admirable, but she's much more concerned for her family than herself. Widowed a few years ago, she was bravely rebuilding her life when cancer struck. Maybe she'll confide in me at some point, we're still getting to know each other, and a relationship needs time to develop. Hopefully, Helen will open up as our relationship grows, and I can be there for her to confide in if she so wishes.

NINE

HELEN

26th September

It is time to address the events from my past which still bring shame and prompt those disturbing nightmares. As weak as we are, there are times we must step up to own our mistakes and attempt to recompense those whom we have wronged. Now is my time, and challenging as it might be, I need to do everything possible to right the terrible wrong I was a part of all those years ago. They say that a drowning man sees his life flash before his eyes in those last few minutes. I can believe there is truth in the saying. However, being in the unenviable position of knowing roughly when my death will occur, has focused my mind on the past, the good and the bad, and I know I must use my remaining time wisely.

As I close my eyes, the panic of that awful evening washes over me again, the screeching of brakes, the thud of contact and Rob shouting in anger at me as I begged him to stop.

Rob Wheeler was precisely the kind of boyfriend my parents would disapprove of, which is why I didn't tell them I was seeing him. He was twenty years old, streetwise and arrogant, an arrogance I then interpreted as confidence and maturity – a potent mix to a sixteen-year-old girl. His brooding dark looks gave him an air of mystery; jet-black hair, worn a little too long and deep brown eyes which had a mesmerising effect on me and many other local girls. Getting out of the house to meet Rob was only possible with the help of my best friend, Susan Wright, who was happy to go along with the lies I told my parents and covered for me if they asked awkward questions.

We thought our clandestine meetings were grown-up. I was besotted with Rob, and his interest in me gave me a certain standing amongst my friends. At just turned sixteen, dating a twenty-year-old was considered cool, and I enjoyed the kudos it brought. My friends were jealous, especially as he had access to his brother's car, which allowed us to go wherever the mood took us. Sometimes Rob's mate came along and Susan would make up a foursome, but on that fateful evening there was only Rob and me.

Memories can be unreliable. The passage of time dulls our recollections, especially if the memories are painful or even shameful, as these most certainly are. Over the years, I've tried not to think about my part in those horrific events, but inevitably something always jogged my memory – made me squirm with the realisation of how weak I was. Not even Andrew knew what happened that night in my youth, it was a secret shame I kept locked in my innermost self, but it was now confronting me – demanding to be redressed.

It was a damp autumn evening, already dark at six o'clock when I left home, telling my parents I was going to Susan's house to do homework. Rob was waiting around the corner, the engine running to heat the car, and I felt the usual rush of excitement at our clandestine meeting. With no plans other than to drive out of town, I kissed him and the smell of alcohol registered in my mind. A brief uncertainty overtook me. If I'd known then what was about to happen, I would never have stayed in the car, but hindsight only emphasises our mistakes, magnifying them in the mind's eye.

I kept silent as Rob drove through the darkened streets heading to the countryside, not wanting to put him into one of his increasingly frequent bad moods. Rob's driving was erratic, but I remained quiet, hoping we would park somewhere not too far away. Today, I can see how much I was afraid of Rob, but our relationship seemed exciting and exhilarating. I was so naïve in thinking I was an adult.

As the car accelerated, my anxiety kept pace, and as we turned a corner rather sharply, a cyclist suddenly appeared ahead of us. It was difficult to make out his figure in the gloomy light and all too quickly there was a loud thud and we swerved into the grass verge, the car stopping abruptly. Rob and I turned in unison to look behind at the tangled mess on the road, which was the cyclist we had hit.

My heart thumped rapidly and I heard the blood pounding in my ears. Instinct made me attempt to get out of the car but Rob caught hold of my arm and pulled me back.

'What do you think you're doing? Get the hell back in. We're out of here!' His voice was loud, angry.

'But he's hurt. He needs help!' Rob ignored my pleas and dragged me back into the car, his vice-like grip hurting my arm. I can't begin to describe how I felt at that moment. I'd seen enough of the cyclist to know he was severely hurt, his body sprawled at an unnatural angle, and his stillness spoke volumes. I trembled with fear but Rob was already manoeuvring the car back onto the road. As we sped off, I tried again to persuade him to turn around and help, or at least to ring for an ambulance, but he growled his refusal and I was too afraid to persist. When Rob eventually stopped the car, he turned to look at me with what seemed like hatred in his eyes.

'You'll tell no one about this, Helen; have you got it, *no one!*'

Rob gripped my shoulders as he spoke, turning me to face him where I could see the raw anger in his dark eyes. Surely there was compassion somewhere in his heart, some remorse at not having stopped, but no, there was nothing, a cold, dark emptiness in his face.

'We should go back, ring for an ambulance...' My words were stopped abruptly by Rob's hand across my cheek, the sting of which released the tears I'd been holding back.

'No! Tonight didn't happen. It was his own stupid fault for being out there in the dark – he deserved it. Now get out, and remember, tell no one!' Rob almost pushed me from the car, and I walked around the block a few times on trembling legs, knowing I couldn't go home in such a state. Within a few minutes, I found myself outside Susan's house. Fortunately, she was the one to answer the doorbell.

'Goodness, what's wrong with you? I thought you were with Rob tonight?'

As I gave way to heaving sobs, Susan ushered me into the hall and up to her bedroom, shouting to her mother, 'It's only Helen – we'll be upstairs.'

Haltingly, I attempted to tell my friend what had happened, knowing Rob would be furious if he found out, but having been confronted by an ugly side of my boyfriend which was far from appealing, I needed to share it with someone. Besides, Susan was my best friend, she'd keep my confidence. When I began to pull myself together, Susan brought a wet flannel from the bathroom to wipe my face. My left cheek stung from Rob's slap, my lip showed signs of swelling and I could taste blood in my mouth. If I didn't see Rob again, it would be too soon.

'What if the man's dead?' I asked. Susan shook her head, unable to answer and almost as shocked as I was. We talked through every possible scenario, none offered a good ending, and dread took hold of me as I trembled.

'He might be okay, and nothing will come of it.' Susan's efforts of comfort didn't sound very convincing.

'You didn't see him! Even in the dark he looked badly hurt – he wasn't moving.'

'Well, there's nothing you can do now unless you want to go to the police?'

'No, I can't do that! What would Mum and Dad say, and Rob?' We talked around and around the issue without deciding anything. Finally, I begged Susan not to tell Rob I'd told her, to which she agreed, apparently every bit afraid of him as I was.

Inevitably, the lies came out of my mouth when I got home. An explanation of my face was necessary, so I said I'd tripped on the way home and bumped my face on a lamp-post. Surprisingly Mum accepted the explanation and brought me an ice pack to help the swelling. As she hugged me, I almost broke down, ashamed of my cowardice and lying to my parents on top of the awful events of the evening.

I didn't sleep much that night. Closing my eyes seemed to propel me back into the car, and the thud of contact banged incessantly in my head like a drum. When morning dawned, I wished it was possible to stay under the blankets and hide from the world, but I knew things must go on as usual to avoid any suspicion. Facing Mum and Dad, I felt sure they'd be able to read what had happened in my cowed expression, but Mum only commented on my swollen face, her sympathy compounding the guilt I already felt.

'Some poor bloke got knocked off his bike last night and killed.' Dad was reading from the local paper. 'A hit and run, they say. I can never understand how someone could do that. If they'd stopped, the man might have been saved.'

Killed. The word stung deeply, cutting through my fraught nerves, and I sat down feeling quite sick.

'Are you all right, love? You look very peaky.' Mum was concerned.

'I'll be fine, just didn't sleep much, that's all.' I forced myself to eat a slice of toast to keep Mum happy.

The news of the accident was quickly forgotten as my parents discussed their favourite subject, our family's imminent move to Sheffield. Dad had been promoted at work and was soon to take up the post of bank manager, a move which was only a month away. I'd dreaded this move for weeks, not wishing to be parted from Rob, but now it couldn't come soon enough. The previous night's events served to open my eyes to Rob's true character, and overnight I'd gone from thinking myself in love with him to being afraid of what he might do.

I made an excuse about needing to be at school early and left the house, feeling sick at the thought of the poor cyclist dead on the road. Images of him lying in a puddle of blood swam through my mind, although it had been too dark to see any blood. Calling for Susan, I was met with a frosty stare. Being early, we went upstairs to her room, where she asked if I'd heard the news. Neither of us knew what to say, but my friend's attitude towards me was not as sympathetic as I'd hoped it might be. Instead, she appeared angry that I'd somehow made her complicit in the lies by telling her. At least she didn't try to persuade me to go to the police again, but there was a barrier between us, an almost tangible coldness when I thought my friend would stand by me and help me to feel better.

We walked to school in uncomfortable silence. Susan spoke only to tell me she would be busy that evening and the coming weekend. My disappointment added to my fear and concern until I turned and ran back home, feeling so overwhelmed with guilt. Susan made no attempt to follow and I couldn't blame her. I was in serious trouble and understood her wanting no part of it. Fortunately, my mother put my feeling unwell down to the fall I'd had the night before and, as it was Friday, said I should stay home and have a quiet day to recover.

Looking back, there were many opportunities to tell my parents – openings I should have taken, but fear of Rob and getting into trouble with the police seemed sufficient reasons not to own up. Even though I kept silent, this incident has remained with me – the biggest mistake and regret of my life. A cowardly act, it has remained in the back of my mind to chastise me when I've been happy, reminding me that I don't deserve happiness and even now, perhaps this is my punishment for past sins. Can I possibly make amends after all this time? All I know is that I must try to do so – there isn't time to delay. The here and now is all I have left – my last chance.

TEN

HELEN

28th September

I grew up in the small mining town of Grimethorpe, sixty miles and a whole lifetime away from the pretty market town where I now live. With no idea where to begin my search, I turned again to my laptop and Google for information. Rob Wheeler may no longer be living in Grimethorpe and it was not a place I wanted to visit again, but if he's still there, I have no choice.

The electoral roll showed an R Wheeler living in Straight Street, the same street Rob's family lived all those years ago. Could it be possible Rob was still in his parents' house? I was unsure whether the ease of finding this information was what I wanted or had I secretly hoped he couldn't be traced. Whatever, it seemed the sensible place to begin, so an early start found me heading towards my hometown, nestled in South Yorkshire, eight miles east of Barnsley. As it was possible to drive there and back in a single day, I wouldn't have to explain an overnight absence to Megan – undoubtedly a plus.

Throughout the journey, my thoughts drifted to those early years spent in Grimethorpe and memories which predominantly brought pain and shame. And now, returning to the scene of my nadir, I wondered how to approach this visit.

We moved away from Grimethorpe shortly after that fateful night and relocated to Castleton. The move was primarily for Dad's job, but I was glad to leave for other reasons by then. I replayed the weeks after the accident in my mind as if it happened only yesterday. Rob was an apprentice motor mechanic in Barnsley while I was at secondary school, so our paths didn't often cross unless by design. After that horrendous night, I didn't want to set eyes on him again, and it appeared he felt the same as he made no effort to contact me. Sadly, it wasn't only Rob who kept out of my way. Susan also grew cold towards me and avoided being with me at school and outside. But I could understand how she felt. I'd involved her in my problem, putting her in a difficult position.

When the hit-and-run victim was named in the paper, it turned out he was a young man who was only recently married. He didn't live in Grimethorpe, so wasn't known personally to us, but the thought of his wife mourning and struggling without him heaped guilt on top of my shame. I loathed myself for my weakness and lived in fear of being found out. There were fruitless appeals for witnesses from the police until eventually the case was no longer reported in the paper as other news filled the front pages. It appeared Rob Wheeler did get away with murder and partly through my cowardice. My fears were real then, and the angry way Rob slapped me ensured my silence even though I knew it was wrong. I was also afraid to tell my parents; they'd trusted me and I'd lied to them each time I met Rob. I couldn't bear to disappoint them. A feeble excuse, yes, but in those frightening dark days there seemed more reasons to keep silent than to own up, and I eventually persuaded myself that I had no choice in the matter. I reasoned that whatever I did couldn't bring the poor man back to his wife, so my silence in some twisted way was valid.

As I approached Grimethorpe my heart rate increased, as if Rob would be there waiting for me – to strike me again, or worse. But my determination was no longer that of a weak teenager but of a grown woman, attempting to right this wrong while there was still time.

The area around me was increasingly familiar. It's a small town, a village which thrived from coal mining in the early eighties when more than half the town's population worked at the pit. However, as the mining industry declined, more and more people struggled to find work and a decade later fifty per cent of the population was unemployed. Grimethorpe was said to be the most deprived town in the country and even in Europe. Such notoriety was balanced by the famous Grimethorpe Colliery Brass Band, featured in the film *Brassed Off*.

As I neared my destination, there were some noticeable changes to my girlhood memories. Government funding for regeneration had been forthcoming and I passed a relatively new housing estate where once a terrace of small miners' cottages stood. For a while, I was confused and couldn't get my bearings but then I came across Straight Street, a terrace of red-brick houses blackened with years of soot. Perhaps they, too, should have been razed to the ground. Some owners had tried to modernise their homes with new double-glazed windows and doors, but these were in the minority. Mostly the houses looked tired, with peeling paintwork and a general uncared-for appearance.

I parked the car at the end of the street, sitting momentarily to collect my thoughts. You may wonder why I wanted to find Rob instead of going straight to the police – the answer was to allow him the opportunity to go to the police first. His confession would surely be better than the police finding out from me. Also, for all I knew, Rob may have changed and lived a decent life since the incident. He would be about sixty-four or five now and was possibly a model citizen.

Being in Grimethorpe, the fear took hold of me again, but what could Rob do to me now? Kill me? It's not much of a threat to a dying woman. I intended to ask him if he would go to the police and confess and if the answer was no then I would go myself. That was the plan, but first I needed to find Rob.

Number 32 was one of the more run-down houses. At some point in its history, the front wall had been pebble-dashed but was now crumbling, with much of it littering the pavement outside the door. The rotting wood around the windows was severely in need of repair and a pane of glass in the front bay had been smashed and covered by inadequate cardboard and masking tape. When I reached for the door knocker, it almost came off in my hand. Again, my heartbeat quickened and my instinct was to turn and run, but I planted my feet firmly on the pavement, willing myself to be strong and ignoring the tight knot of fear in my chest. Eventually, the door was pulled halfway open and an old lady squinted into my face. A gnarled, arthritic hand rested on a walking stick which she raised almost accusingly and asked, 'What do you want?'

My mind whirred; I was reminded of Miss Havisham in *Great Expectations*. She may be old, but the way she grasped the stick made me take a step backwards. If this was Rob's mother, she must be well into her eighties, possibly pushing ninety.

'Mrs Wheeler?' I asked.

'And who wants to know?'

'My name's Helen and I'm looking for Rob Wheeler. We were friends when we were younger.' *Friends* would hardly describe how we parted.

A man's voice shouted from inside. 'Who is it, Ma?'

I gasped. Could it be Rob? Was he still living here with his mother? A shadow appeared behind Mrs Wheeler. I tried to see him better but the sun behind me cast shadows in the hallway, hampering my vision. When he stepped forward, I stared, incredulous. This man's age was about right; the youthful black hair now liberally peppered with grey and thinning on top. Yes, it must be him. I mumbled his name.

'And what would you want if I was Rob Wheeler?' He stepped forward, head tilted to one side, a curious expression on his face. I could see then how the years had not been kind to him. He was much heavier than in his youth – stomach bulging over his belt and at least a few days' stubble on his chin. Dark eyebrows almost met over his eyes, giving him a menacing scowl which made me want to turn and run. However, having come this far, I remained determined to continue my mission.

'It's a rather personal matter. Could we talk somewhere more private?'

'You'd better come in then.' He pulled the door open and I reluctantly followed through the hall. A smell of damp lingered in the air, mingled with another more unpleasant odour which I couldn't quite place. He led me in while his mother followed on and sat on a rather grubby armchair. I looked around; the room appeared frozen in time from the day the family first moved in. A threadbare carpet barely covered the floorboards, thick dust lay on everything, and stale tobacco filled the air. I looked at Rob, then at his mother, trying to somehow communicate that this was not something we could discuss in her presence. Two identical pairs of deep brown eyes were focused on me, making me quite uneasy. I had to say something but what? Suddenly the old lady laughed out loud.

'Come on, son,' she said with a wry smile, 'put the lass out of her misery and tell her!'

I was confused; tell me what, I wondered. He laughed too.

'Rob doesn't live here anymore. I'm Ricky, his brother.'

Taking a deep breath, I sat down before my legs gave way. 'You could have told me straight away.' I spoke quietly, without the energy even to raise my voice. Mother and son were still laughing at my expression. She spoke next.

'Rob still lives locally, on the swanky new estate back up the hill. Do you want Ricky to ring him for you?'

'No, thanks. If you give me the address, I'll find my own way there.'

'What's it all about then?' Ricky grinned at my discomfort. 'Don't tell me he's got another girl into trouble. Your daughter, is it?'

'It's nothing of the sort, and I'd rather discuss it with your brother.' I rose to leave and the old lady recited an address, a street I'd never heard of. I couldn't get out of there quickly enough and walked briskly back to the car, where I sat for a few minutes, trembling. They were probably ringing Rob to warn him of a maniac who was looking for him, but I no longer cared. Hopefully, I would see him today to allow him the opportunity to go to the police before I did. One thing I was sure about was that Rob Wheeler would not welcome my visit.

Hazel Avenue was easy enough to find even from such vague directions. It was one of the newly-built houses I'd passed on my way into Grimethorpe – an expansive tree-lined cul-de-sac in which Rob's house occupied the head. Although not far in distance, it was a world away from those terraces I remembered from childhood. Again, I left my car relatively far from the house and walked to number 18. As I rang the doorbell, my expectations were low after the experience at Rob's mother's house, although from the outside, this was the finest house on the estate, modern, detached and with a double garage to one side. I found it hard to imagine Rob living here after meeting his mother and brother.

No one appeared to be home, and I was tempted to retreat to the safety of my car and consider other possible ways of contacting him. A letter perhaps? I rang again and heard, with mixed feelings, the sound of someone coming to open the door. Having steeled myself to come face to face with Rob, it was a surprise to see a woman half-hidden by the door as she peered suspiciously at me.

'I was hoping to see Rob. Is he in?' The woman shook her head but remained at the door, staring curiously at me.

'Could you tell me when he'll be back?' I hated the thought of waiting but no more than the thought of coming back another day, the lesser of two evils perhaps.

'You don't remember me, do you?' the half-hidden woman asked. Looking closely at her face there was something familiar.

'Come in, Helen, and you can tell me why you want to see my husband.'

As the door opened wider, I could see the woman clearer: Susan Wright! My childhood best friend was now so changed that I'd have passed her by in the street without recognition. She'd put on at least a couple of stones in weight, and her hair was dyed a brassy blonde, frizzy from too many perms. She bore no resemblance to the sixteen-year-old fresh-faced girl I'd known. Following her into the house, I needed to stop myself from staring. The Susan I remembered was pretty with naturally blonde hair, slim and always immaculately turned out. This woman looked far older than me, with sagging skin dragging her features down, but even more of a surprise – she'd referred to Rob as her husband!

The house's interior was well-proportioned with an open-plan living area and French windows leading to an immaculate garden. And it was extravagantly furnished, with leather sofas, black-glass coffee and lamp tables and a vast wall-mounted television dominating the room. From the outside, I judged the house would have at least four bedrooms, which made me wonder if they had family living at home. For all the fancy furnishings, the predominant feature was a strong smell of cat pee.

'I'd never have guessed it was you when Ricky said a woman was coming. I didn't expect ever to see you again. So why are you here, Helen? Don't tell me you have hopes of a loving reconciliation with Rob!' Susan was laughing at me. Her features appeared hardened, she looked much older than her sixty years, and her voice had taken on the gravelly timbre of a heavy smoker. When she waved a hand at a seat, I took it as an invitation and sat on a huge leather armchair. Susan sat beside a ginger cat on the sofa and stroked his back. I ignored her comment.

'I didn't know you married Rob – it's quite a surprise.' My words were out before I thought about them.

'How would you have known? But it's none of your business anyway!' Susan's body language was defensive, her chin held high, her eyes narrow. True, it was none of my business, and I didn't wish to sit there making small talk any more than she did.

'Will Rob be back soon?' I ventured.

'Maybe, maybe not.' She shrugged. 'What's it about then?'

It seemed pointless to keep the purpose of my visit from her; after all, Susan knew everything about that night.

'I intend to go to the police and report the incident when the man on his bike was killed.'

Susan's jaw dropped. 'But you can't do that! Why on earth would you want to anyway?' Her voice was raised.

'It's stayed with me, Susan, something I can never forget. I should have gone to the police then, I remember you suggested it, but I was afraid.'

'Well, you should be bloody afraid now too! If Rob hears you say that – well, I wouldn't want to be in your shoes!'

I was saved from having to answer by a mobile phone ringing. Susan picked it up and smiled when she saw the caller ID. From the one side of the conversation I could hear, it was Rob asking who their unexpected visitor was. Susan told him my name and then laughed at the response. Closing the phone, she turned to me. 'He's on his way.'

I was naturally apprehensive but also relieved. Hopefully, this could be a one-time visit. Returning another day was not something I relished, and the thought of meeting Rob Wheeler again still made me shudder. It seemed likely that Rob made himself scarce when his brother rang to say someone was looking for him, and Susan had now given him the okay to return home. From the window, I saw a black Lexus pull onto the drive, and Rob Wheeler stepped out, his feet crunching across the gravel.

The front door banged, making me jump.

'Well, well, well, look who's come to visit – and after all this time!' Rob sneered rather than spoke. I was as unwelcome to him as to Susan. Time had not been kind to Rob either. His once-black hair was almost entirely grey and worn rather long over his collar. He, too, had gained weight, and if ever his features had been attractive, they were far from it now. A rather bulbous red nose suggested someone who drank too much, and from the colour of his pudgy fingers, he was also a heavy smoker. As if to confirm this, Rob took a packet of cigarettes from his pocket and lit one up. There was a striking resemblance to his brother, except Rob wore better-quality clothes. He scooped the cat off the sofa and sat down next to Susan. My instincts were crying out to escape their house as quickly as possible, but having come so far, I needed to say my piece. Susan, however, beat me to it.

'She's talking about going to the police, Rob.'

'About what?' Rob adopted an exaggerated puzzled look, acting as if he had no idea as to what she referred to.

'I want to make amends for my part in the accident... when the cyclist was killed.' I hoped Rob didn't detect the tremor in my voice. I wanted to sound confident and in control.

'What cyclist? I haven't a clue what you're talking about.' Rob smiled as he spoke, deliberately goading me, acting innocent, which all three of us knew he was not.

'It's played on my conscience for years, and I know it was a long time ago, but it might bring his wife some peace to know precisely what happened.' As I spoke, Rob scratched his head, glancing from me to Susan.

'Do you know what she's talking about? Because I certainly don't.'

'Haven't a clue, Rob. She's barmy if you ask me.' Susan played along, and I feared my visit had been in vain. It was time to go. I didn't want to be in their company any longer but I gave him one last chance.

'I came to you first to allow you time to go to the police before I do. If you confess, they're more likely to be lenient, so I'll wait a couple of days, and if I don't hear from you, I'll be going to the police myself.' My voice was cracking with emotion. I had to get out – breathing in there was increasingly difficult. I stood up – Rob sprang to his feet, blocking the doorway.

'Don't you come here giving me ultimatums! If you go telling the cops anything, you'll regret it. Understand?' His face was uncomfortably close – I could smell the alcohol and nicotine on his breath. I stepped back and flung a piece of paper with a mobile phone number onto the seat I'd just vacated.

'You can ring me on this number.' I could say no more and pushed myself past Rob Wheeler to escape his house.

My legs trembled so much that I felt in danger of falling flat on my face, yet somehow, I reached the car, scrambled inside and locked the door. It was several minutes until I could drive, and even now, writing this account brings back a crippling sense of fear. The only thing left for me to do was to wait – for two very long days.

ELEVEN
HELEN

29th September

After a surprisingly good night's sleep, I awoke to the sound of birds in the trees outside and the distant barking of a dog, reminding me there were still good things in my life. The sun, too, was attempting to make an appearance, a more than welcome sight after a couple of grey overcast days. Gus's tail thumped on the bed, his usual morning greeting, and he received the fuss he'd come to expect as his right. Getting up, I let him out into the garden before filling the kettle to make tea. It was a good morning as far as pain was concerned and my spirits, too, were far better than yesterday. Perhaps this was due to having succeeded in making the first step towards a degree of recompense for past mistakes. I looked at the mobile phone on the kitchen table and wondered if it would ring today, tomorrow, or not at all.

The phone thing was maybe a tad overdramatic, I've probably watched too many detective films, but I needed some way for Rob to contact me without giving away my address or landline number. It's an old pay-as-you-go which I found in the drawer after Andrew died. He'd rarely used it, but there was still some credit on it, and it occurred to me how it could be helpful in my quest and afterwards, I could throw it away. Unfortunately, staring at it wouldn't make it ring, so I turned away, determined not to think about the subject for the next two days and spend my time doing something pleasurable instead.

Telephoning Megan was always good and we agreed to meet in town for coffee while Sam was at nursery and after picking him up we'd decide what to do for the afternoon. So, an hour and a half later, my daughter and I were seated in the corner of our favourite coffee shop.

'I tried to ring you yesterday, Mum, but you must have been out?' This was clearly a question to which an explanation was required.

'I went for a long drive to relive some old memories, but I'm all yours today, so what shall we do with Sam this afternoon?' I hated deceiving Megan, yet didn't want to tell her what I was doing either – perhaps in the hope I may never have to.

'Sam would enjoy the park if it's not too cold for you, then we can go to the café for coffee and a warm-up. How decadent, coffee out twice in one day!'

'It suits me fine. I feel like being lazy today, and who better to share the day with than you and Sam.'

'So, tell me more about Canada. Did you bring the photographs?'

I spent the next half hour showing my daughter where her brother lived and all the places they'd taken me to. We pored over the images, all else forgotten for those precious few minutes.

'Ethan looks so much like Sam – they could be brothers rather than cousins.' Megan was correct, there was a strong resemblance. It's a shame they lived so far apart, they could have been such good friends.

'Why don't you and James take Sam over there next year?

Luke would love to have you and the boys could spend time together?' I know she missed her brother, they'd been so close as children.

'It's such an expense and we're trying to save up to move to a bigger house.' Megan sounded wistful. I knew they'd dearly love another baby too, but it didn't seem to be happening, and the plan had always been to move when they could afford it.

'Well, you'll be coming into money by next summer, love. You could use that.' It was perhaps tactless to be so blunt, but there'd be a hefty insurance payment and the house when I died.

'Mum, don't say such things. I want you around as long as possible!' Tears welled up in Megan's eyes.

'I'm sorry, love, but it's a fact... and I'd like nothing more than to know you'll be able to visit Luke and move to a bigger house when the time comes.'

My daughter frowned and returned to the photographs of my trip to Canada. I chatted about each image to show her something of the area and take her mind off my clumsy, thoughtless words.

Picking Sam up from nursery was always a delight. We watched through the glass panel in the classroom door, witnessing his joy as he played with the sand tray with two friends.

'That's George and Ellie. Sam talks non-stop about them – his best friends or buddies as he calls them. Hopefully, they'll all attend the same school next year or Sam will be broken-hearted.' Megan sighed.

'He seems so young for school, childhood passes far too quickly.' A clear mental image of my children's first day at school made me smile. Being twins they were fortunate enough to have each other to lean on, but there was still the odd tearful day, mainly from Megan who was such a shy child. There were often mornings when strange ailments were invented, which she hoped would be severe enough to let her stay at home with me. One day her hair was 'hurting' so badly, she insisted she couldn't go to school. Another time Megan put red spots all over her face with a marker pen and told me Miss had said they couldn't go to school if they had the 'chicken spots' or the other children might catch it. It's strange the memories we keep stored away, events which make us smile but sadly can never be relived, no matter how much we wish to do so. I was so proud of my children; their childhood days were long and perfect, filled with laughter and love – a time I thought would last forever but soon learned it was only fleeting. What passes us by can never be replaced; time moves in only one direction, which sadly is forward. Yet I have armfuls of memories which flood my mind as I write this journal.

Sam spotted us watching and ran to the door, his little face beaming excitedly.

'Grandma, this is George and this is Ellie!' he announced with a flourish. He must have told me this at least a dozen times, but I duly said hello to his friends then goodbye as we took Sam home.

After lunch, we trundled to the park where I watched my grandson race around squealing with excitement, fearlessly using the swings and slide and scrambling up the climbing frame. Each day I concentrate on making new memories which will stay with me for a short time but are no less precious.

Once back home, I looked at the phone, still on the kitchen table where I'd left it. Picking it up to check for voicemails brought mixed feelings when there were none. Did I want to hear from Rob Wheeler, or did I want to go directly to the police without further contact?

Go straight to jail and do not pass go!

I shivered, ambivalent as to which outcome was preferable.

Tired and cold, I ran a hot bath and soaked away my cares, at least for the moment. Tomorrow would come in its own good time. I was in no hurry for any tomorrows now – the days of wishing time away were long behind me.

30th September

I'm beginning to wish I still had a job to go to, which would at least be a productive distraction. I know this restless feeling is because today's the day Rob might ring. If he doesn't, I must follow through with my resolve and go to the police alone. Did I not write only yesterday that I don't wish my days away? Yet here I am longing for this day to end and perhaps the next day, too. What could I do to keep occupied? I could do more in the garden while the weather holds but my heart isn't in it, and I only ever do what's necessary to keep it tidy.

Although I'm always welcome at Megan's, I don't want her to feel she must include me in every aspect of her life. We spent yesterday together, a gloriously simple day of idle chatter, enjoying Sam and drinking too much coffee, so today I'll be alone. Many people would envy this time I have to myself, but there are only so many books you can read, and I refuse to succumb to daytime television. At least with the weather holding, Gus and I can get out for long walks, which will do us both good.

We did walk for over an hour and came back exhausted, at least I was. Gus had enough energy to run around all day. With coffee and a chocolate biscuit (not having a future to worry about has a few advantages, one of which is not caring about gaining weight!) I put my feet on the sofa and rested my head on the cushion.

In my mind's eye, I imagined Luke and Megan as children

again. Two fair heads conspiratorially locked together as they played in the garden during all weathers. Summers were long and golden, a paddling pool cooling hot skin and bringing opportunities to drench each other and me if I was too close – a see-saw balanced by siblings of equal weight – two swings to compete for who dared to go the highest – picnics on the lawn, or in a tent made from a clothes-horse and a sheet. Winters brought snowball fights and competitions for the best-dressed snowman. Hats and scarves vanished from their shelves until the snow melted, and the snowmen were no more. When Megan and Luke were young, there were shared birthday parties which turned into sleepovers or video nights as they grew older, and I soon learned that one cake would never do and always baked two to each of my children's specifications.

Closing my eyes and rubbing Gus's ears, I could picture Andrew, tall and handsome, laughing as he carried Luke on his back and Megan under his arm, to shouts of, 'Faster, Daddy, faster' before they collapsed in a heap on the grass. They were days we thought would never end. Family holidays, school sports days, and Christmas nativity plays were all eventually replaced by exams, university, engagements and weddings. When did Andrew and I become the older generation? Our parents all lived to see their grandchildren, but only my mother is alive now, and on occasions when I look into the mirror, I see her face looking back at me. When Andrew's brow furrowed in concentration, he was the image of his father. Now when I watch Sam, I can see his mother in how he twists his hair when he's tired, and when I first heard Ethan laugh, it could have been Luke thirty years ago. The family bonds are strengthened by love, and I hope my children and grandchildren will have happy and fulfilled lives, even though I will not be around to witness them.

TWELVE
HELEN

1st October

My family have had time to get used to the idea that I'll not be with them for much longer. Now it is time to tell my circle of friends, and this afternoon will present the opportunity to do so. I know this reluctance to talk to people is silly, yet I feel a strong desire to protect those I love from the hurt this news will bring. When Andrew died, I was blessed by the understanding of several good friends and family who helped to lift me back into some semblance of normality with their love and kindness. I owe these friends so much and so it's time to tell them the truth.

About once a month I meet for coffee with four of my closest friends to catch up on each other's news. Today is the day, and it is my turn to open my home to our close-knit little group. We've been friends since our children were small, having met at the usual toddler groups and the school gate. Marie, Sarah and Pam still live locally, while Jennie moved to a village not too far away and always makes an effort to travel the forty miles or so for our monthly get-together. Between us, we have eleven children, all of whom are grown up and living independently, except for Marie's youngest son, Adrian. He was born with cerebral palsy and Down's syndrome, a cruel double whammy. Of the five of us, I admire Marie the most. Her older son, Peter, is the same age as Megan and Luke, and we were already firm friends when Adrian was born. Tests in early pregnancy flagged up warnings of his health problems but there was no way Marie and her husband, Brian, would consider a termination. For them, Adrian's life began at conception, and he was loved no less because of the doctor's diagnosis. We all admire them greatly for their courage.

As a group of young mothers, we supported each other through the pitfalls of child-rearing, comparing notes and sharing milestones, even down to forming a cartel to set the going rate for the tooth fairy! We celebrated bonfire night together, pooled our fireworks for a better display and hosted regular sleepovers for the children, allowing us to have a social life as adults. We even had a successful chicken-pox party one year. Our children bonded too and are still friends today, most of them repeating the cycle with their own young children. Our meetings are always full of laughter and fun – we rarely talk of serious matters such as death, but these dear friends deserve to know. We've helped each other through difficult times, and my impending death will be no exception.

Jennie arrived first and followed me into the kitchen where I was buttering scones and setting a tray for coffee.

'Have you lost weight, Helen? You look so much slimmer – those trousers are almost dropping off you.'

I smiled and agreed – yes, I had lost weight recently. The doorbell rang again and Marie and Pam came in together with Sarah parking her car just behind them. As they were all busy greeting each other I left them in the lounge to finish making the coffee. Jennie joined me again, and I asked if she'd carry the tray. Picking it up, she looked at me with concern but said nothing. It didn't take much scrutiny to see I was not well, even with the make-up I'd carefully applied. Suddenly I felt weak and inadequate and to my embarrassment, tears flowed down my cheeks. Jennie put the tray down and hugged me as I tried to stem the flow, to be brave even though I felt anything but.

'You're not well, are you?' Jennie asked softly.

'No.' The single word almost choked me. We heard a sudden shriek of laughter from the lounge and I pulled myself together, smiling at my perceptive friend and dabbing my eyes with a tissue. Jennie carried the tray through to the lounge. I wanted to wait until we'd caught up on each other's lives before telling them my news, but red eyes and a tear-stained face gave me away.

'Helen, what's wrong? You look awful,' Pam blurted out.

'Thanks for that, Pam.' Her typical bluntness made me smile. Dressing the news up was pointless, so I came straight out with it and watched my friends' expressions change as they took in my words.

'But aren't you having chemotherapy or something? Treatment is so advanced these days,' Sarah enquired. I shook my head.

'It was too far gone when they found it – nothing can be done. It's only a matter of time.'

'Bloody hell, Helen, how terrible!' Pam exclaimed loudly as usual, forthright and to the point. Jennie and Marie stayed silent, their faces solemn and tongues stilled by the awful news.

'How long have you got?' Pam was the spokeswoman again, asking the question which was on all of their minds.

'I should be all right until Christmas, at least I hope so and next year who knows? It's difficult to predict exactly how long my body can resist the spread of the cancer.'

'But that's only three months away; how awful!' Jennie looked truly saddened.

'Well, I think we should do something about this. Forget the coffee, Helen, have you anything stronger? No, stuff that too. Why don't we go out and have the wake now while Helen's still with us?' Pam's words gave us something else to think about and laughter suddenly bubbled up inside me. What a deliciously wicked idea!

'Yes, I'd rather enjoy going to my wake, you know, to hear what you all have to say about me! But it's my treat, and we'll go to the new country club at the west end of town, Grange Lodge, isn't it? Come on, drink your coffee while I ring to see if they can accommodate us for lunch.'

'But I'm not dressed for somewhere swanky,' Sarah grumbled, which was nonsense as she was always immaculately turned out.

'With those Gianvito Rossi shoes, you'll be allowed in anywhere. Just wave your Vivienne Westwood bag under the concierge's nose, it'll be fine!' Pam grinned as I picked up the phone. The idea captured me. The spontaneity was alluring and I suddenly felt like celebrating, and what better thing to celebrate than my own life?

The Lodge could take us for lunch in The Orangery at twelve thirty, enough time to finish our coffee and pile into Pam's four-by-four to set off on our crazy quest.

'I've never eaten quail's eggs before,' admitted Jennie as we pored over the menu in the rather grand Orangery. 'It's quite expensive, Helen. Are you sure we can't pay for our own?'

'Certainly not. If you want to do this again when I'm gone, then do so and pay for yourselves, but for now, as I'm the one whose wake this is, I'll pay.' The young waiter heard this nugget of conversation and almost dropped the basket of bread he was offering around the table.

'Yes,' I told him, 'we are having a wake, but take no notice. At our age, we're all more than a little senile.' The young man smiled weakly and hastily went to refill the water jug, which was still three-quarters full. We were quiet for a minute or two as we decided what to eat and gave our order to the young girl who'd appeared at our table – I think we'd scared her colleague off. It felt wonderfully indulgent to be there in the middle of the week and order such extravagant food, and my earlier mood dispersed to be replaced by a devil-may-care attitude.

As we waited for our meal, the conversation became more general. Marie updated us on how Adrian was. They felt the time had come to look at residential care for him, not that they wanted him to leave home, but his future needed to be settled. As Marie and Brian aged, their concern for their son increased, knowing caring for him at home wasn't possible forever. It was a difficult decision, but finding a place while they were still around for the transition period made sense. Perhaps my situation validated how none of us will be here for our children forever.

Jennie pressed me for details of my visit to Canada; it was now clear why I'd decided to go at what must have appeared to be very short notice. I described the township where Luke and Imogen lived and the amazing scenery. And then I told them about Ethan and how we'd skimmed pebbles into the sea and walked barefoot along the beach. I thought about Tim and wondered if I should tell my friends about him. But decided not to. That strange and wonderful encounter was something precious which I wanted to keep to myself for the moment. I felt like a child, hugging the memories tightly to my chest like a comfort blanket. They probably thought my smiles were brought about by remembering my family, and I wasn't about to correct them.

We chattered through the first and main courses, each limiting ourselves to one glass of wine, me because of medication and my friends because they were driving. When dessert was served, a deliciously mouth-watering lemon cheesecake with cherry sorbet, Pam decided we should have a toast.

'This has been a wonderful occasion. We met to share coffee and gossip, yet found ourselves enjoying a sumptuous meal courtesy of our dear friend, Helen. We've helped each other through good times and bad, and I know we all feel a bond due to those shared times. Helen's news has, in equal measure, shocked and saddened us, but it's good to share with her today, to relive old memories and appreciate her while she's still with us. Please lift your glasses to toast our wonderful, brave friend, Helen Reid.' They did as asked and I raised my glass to four of the best friends I could ever have had.

Later in the day, reflecting on the time with my 'girls', I was surprised at how happy it made me feel. Perhaps we should all attend our own wake on reaching a certain age; I'd found the experience quite uplifting and decided there and then I would leave my friends a thousand pounds each and stipulate that they do this again, in memory of me.

The spontaneity of it all was exactly what I needed – to get out of the house and do something different stopped me from torturing myself with thoughts of Rob Wheeler. He'd not invaded my mind for several hours, although when I arrived home, I couldn't resist checking the phone for messages. There were none. Maybe later tonight or tomorrow? Perhaps he was trying to scare me by leaving it to the very last minute. I don't know, but I do know I have some wonderful caring friends. They all made me promise to call them if I needed help or simply just a shoulder to cry on, and we parted as if having attended an enjoyable party together, which in a way was precisely what it had been.

THIRTEEN
HELEN

2nd October

The phone call never came. Either Rob assumed I was bluffing, or his arrogance would not allow him to confess to his long-ago crime. The only thing left for me to do was go to the police by myself.

The nearest manned police station to Grimethorpe was in Barnsley, and I was on the road by eight in the morning, wanting my task to be over with as soon as possible. As the satnav spewed out monotonous directions, I tried hard to concentrate on the road and stop my thoughts from racing ahead. It was raining, almost torrential at times, and the wipers worked furiously to clear the windscreen, their rhythmic action almost mesmerising.

By ten o'clock, I was driving past the police station, searching for a parking spot close enough so I wouldn't be soaked to the skin when I went inside. Sitting in the car for a few minutes to compose myself, I watched the rain coursing down the windows and wished this ordeal was over. There was so much I couldn't predict about what would happen, so many questions swimming in my mind, and I felt totally alone. It wasn't something I could talk to anyone about, and to take such a massive step as this without sharing it with someone close was frightening, but shame prevented me from seeking another opinion. Finally, the rain eased off somewhat and taking an umbrella from the boot, I locked the car and set off towards the police station.

Having never been in such a place before, I was more than a little apprehensive about what would happen. Should I have rung beforehand to make an appointment? It was all so confusing and almost laughable that someone would ring and make an appointment to confess to a crime. If there was any protocol for this kind of thing it was lost on me.

Stepping around puddles and hurrying along the street, I soon arrived at the sixties-built station. It was an angular sprawling building with sharp corners, concrete and steel, a flat roof and glazed doorways. Pushing open the heavy, squeaking door and walking through, I thought it could have been any office building. A reception desk immediately opposite the entrance was flanked by swing doors leading to corridors, presumably with rooms on each side. It was stark and unwelcoming, but why would it be welcoming? I was certainly out of my comfort zone here. Perspex screened the reception desk, and I briefly wondered if it was bulletproof. I apparently didn't look threatening as an officer slid open a panel in the screen to talk to me. My mouth was suddenly dry, and the words I'd rehearsed disappeared into the turmoil which was my mind.

'I... I'd like to speak to someone about a crime.' It was the best I could manage. The very polite constable smiled and asked a few questions, working to draw out from me what he needed to know to determine the appropriate officer for me to see. I was asked to wait and directed to a row of orange plastic bucket seats against the far wall, where I sat squirming with shame and embarrassment whilst my request was considered.

A young man was seated at the other end of the row, head in his hands and elbows resting on his knees. He seemed even more agitated than I was, tapping his foot furiously on the floor. Tattoos covered both his forearms, intricate designs which appeared to run together into an indefinable inky mass. Piercings littered his face and ears, some of which looked quite painful. Trying to imagine why he was there diverted my attention from my reasons for all of thirty seconds, and then I took a deep breath to try and relax my tense body. Finally, one pair of swing doors opened and a uniformed officer came through; my heart skipped a beat.

'Jason.' He spoke just one word and nodded to the young man, who stood immediately and followed through the swing doors with a swagger which belied his nervousness. I relaxed a little.

A mother came in, jiggling a baby on one hip with a toddler holding her free hand. I watched as she went to the desk and rapped impatiently on the screen. When it opened, the woman shouted obscenities at the officer, using such awful language that I cringed. It was hard not to hear what she was saying, but a policewoman soon appeared and took the lady away through the second set of doors. Others arrived and the entrance area began to fill up. I really did not want to be there, but it was too late to back out now.

Twenty minutes passed before someone came to me, minutes when I struggled to prevent myself from getting up and running away from what now seemed like such a bad idea. A tall man, probably in his late thirties, stood before me and spoke my name. I jumped up almost as quickly as the young man had and dutifully followed him through the doors and down a corridor.

The room he took me into was stuffy and stark, furnished with a small table and four chairs, two on either side. The only window was frosted glass, and the room was lit by a fluorescent tube which flickered noisily when switched on. Grey walls made the room feel grubby, and the vinyl floor covering was streaked with rubber smears, presumably from the rubber feet of the chairs. The officer introduced himself as Detective Sergeant Simon Greenwood, and we were quickly joined by DC Rose Hamilton. They smiled politely, but I could sense a curiosity in their expressions and wondered how much the desk officer had passed on. Finally, the DS opened the dialogue.

'I understand you wish to report a crime – a historic one?'

'Yes,' I answered, barely recognising the feeble, shaky voice coming from my mouth.

'Can you tell me how long ago we're talking about?' A reasonable request and I knew the answer was somewhere in my mind. I'd rehearsed this over and over a thousand times.

'1970,' I replied.

'And were you a witness to this crime or a participant?' The detective drew in a deep breath, probably thinking this would take a long time if every answer had to be dragged from me.

'Both. I mean – it was an accident. I was a passenger in the car when a man was knocked over and killed.' My face felt hot and I must have been the colour of beetroot. The room seemed devoid of air, stuffy to the extreme.

'Did you not give a statement at the time of this accident?' His brown eyes looked quizzically into mine. The DC sitting beside him held a pen over a notepad, poised to write something when I eventually gave them something coherent to record.

'We, he... my boyfriend at the time, didn't stop, we argued and he drove away. I tried to get him to go back but he threatened me.' Was this making sense? I pulled back my shoulders, breathed deeply and attempted to offer a sensible account. 'It was October the twentieth 1970 at about seven pm. Rob picked me up in the car and we drove out of town. He was driving too fast – it was dark and he didn't see the man as we drove round the bend until it was too late. I tried to make him stop, to go back, but he refused and when he drove me home, Rob made it clear I was to tell no one. It wasn't until the next day that I learned the man had died.' I stopped to draw breath and noticed DC Hamilton had made a few notes – from what I could see, it was the date and time. DS Greenwood stood up to leave the room, taking the notepad. The policewoman offered to fetch me a glass of water which I accepted gratefully, and I found myself alone in the room, feeling nervous and ashamed. When she returned I thanked her, and as we waited, she explained how the DS had gone to run the date I'd given through the computer. It made sense. Neither of these officers would have been born so long ago, but there would surely be details of the unsolved crime recorded somewhere.

When the sergeant returned some twenty minutes later, he carried a thin sheaf of paper and looked solemn. He pushed the papers towards his colleague for her to read and turned his attention to me.

'You mentioned Rob. What was his full name?'

'Wheeler, Rob Wheeler.' I thought I detected a flicker of recognition at the name.

'And can you tell me why you never reported this incident at the time?'

'I was frightened. Rob hit me and made it clear I was to tell no one about the events of the night. I was only sixteen and very afraid, and I suppose I didn't want my parents to know I'd been with him either. They thought I was with a friend, doing homework.' It was as if I was reliving the evening again, and I could almost feel the sting on my cheek from Rob's slap. The DC continued to write while the DS kept his eyes on me as if deciding whether I was telling the truth.

'And did you tell anyone?' he continued.

'Yes. I went to my friend's house, Susan. I told her everything and she said I should go to the police, but then we decided that the man may not have been hurt, so it might not matter. It was something like that – it's so long ago and I don't remember all the details.'

'And what was Susan's surname?'

'Wright, she was the same age as me, sixteen, but she's Rob's wife now. I was surprised to see her with him.'

'Could you tell me, Helen, why have you come forward now after such a long time?'

I didn't want to tell them about the cancer, I needed to keep some dignity in this situation and not use my illness as an excuse, so I answered truthfully without disclosing everything.

'It's always troubled me and recently even more so. I've begun to have nightmares and flashbacks, so I'd like to do the right thing.'

'But you didn't want to do the right thing then?' The detective sounded harsh, which was no more than I deserved. The DC glanced in his direction, maybe a little surprised at his tone. I looked down at my hands in my lap and answered, 'No.'

'The man who died was only twenty-three and had been married a few months earlier.' DS Greenwood seemed intent on making me squirm, and it was working. Then, after a moment's silence, he spoke again.

'What happens now is that we'll take a few more details and then fix a time for you to come back and give a full statement which will be videotaped.' He gathered the papers and stood to leave. I wanted to stop him, to say I couldn't come back another time. I needed to get it over with as soon as possible, but he was out of the room before I could speak. The DC smiled at me, a little comfort after her sergeant's cold words.

'Can I take your full name and address?' she asked, pen poised over the pad.

'Could we possibly get all this over with today?' I asked. 'It might be difficult for me to come back.'

'Look, Helen, we have procedures for this kind of thing. We need to make arrangements to take a video statement.'

I should have expected this. Looking into the young woman's pale-blue eyes, I could discern a caring heart. I was confessing to my part in a crime, but somehow this girl before me seemed to understand how difficult this was, even though I deserved no understanding. The DS was probably right in his attitude to me, considering what that poor man's wife must have gone through. Perhaps I needed to be completely honest and tell them why I had to do this as soon as possible.

'I'd hoped to make an official statement today. I've been unwell lately with terminal cancer, and I often don't know how I'll be or what I'll be able to do from one day to the next.'

The constable's face reflected a kindness I didn't deserve, almost making me cry.

'Look, can you wait here a little longer and I'll have a word with the DS to see what we can do?'

I smiled my thanks and was again left alone in that awful room with only my thoughts for company, thoughts I didn't want to entertain. Ten minutes passed before Rose Hamilton returned to sit opposite me.

'If you could manage this afternoon, we can set things up for about two. Would that be any help? It's eleven thirty now, so you can wait here if you like, or perhaps find somewhere to have a coffee and something to eat.'

I couldn't bear two and a half hours in that room, so I opted for the latter suggestion and, after thanking her for arranging things, left the police station for a much-needed break. The rain had stopped, and walking back to the car, I noticed a café almost opposite the car park, not a particularly salubrious one but undoubtedly preferable to the police station. After stopping at a newsagent to buy a magazine, I went into the café and ordered a coffee, unsure if I could drink it and certainly unable to stomach any food.

Undoubtedly it had been an embarrassing and painful morning, but at least it would be all over on the same day. I should have expected having to return later and was grateful for the trouble they were taking to allow this to happen today. I knew I didn't deserve any concessions and hadn't wanted to disclose my illness, but it was a practical consideration. I no longer had the luxury of planning too far ahead.

With twenty minutes to spare, I returned to the police station, having drunk two cups of weak, milky coffee and still feeling tired, as if I'd run a marathon. Hoping this wouldn't take long (I wanted to avoid travelling home in the rush hour), I took the same seat in the reception area. Trying to use the time constructively, I planned exactly what to say and reckoned sticking to the facts would be the best way to get it over quickly.

The human mind tends to relate historic episodes in a way which puts the narrator in a good light, but I could think of nothing good about that particular episode. Still, it was tempting to try and lay all the blame on Rob, as if I'd had no choice in the matter. The fact is, I did have a choice – I could have told my parents or gone to the police. Doing neither simply compounded the whole incident. Police time was wasted and the victim's family must have suffered enormously as the investigation dragged on and was never resolved, and it had done me no good either. If I'd done the right thing at the time, this scenario would not now be playing out. It may not have been easy to own up all those years ago but it would be over and

I wouldn't be reliving it today. My silence then was unforgivable – is it too late to make amends?

Recording my statement felt somewhat unreal. DS Greenwood asked me to retell my story just as I'd done earlier in the day and try to ignore the camera, which didn't seem too intrusive. The sergeant was perhaps a little friendlier than earlier, which made me think the DC must have told him about my illness. I was grateful – feelings of being no better than a criminal had haunted me for years, and I didn't need to be treated like one. No one could be more disgusted with me than I was with myself.

Managing to get across the details of the evening as honestly and accurately as possible, I hoped my memory served me well. The video camera ran for the whole time of the interview, and only when it was finally switched off did I relax, having been tense throughout with an increasingly bad headache and a searing pain in my back. Before allowing me to go, DC Hamilton told me they'd keep me informed about their investigation, something which still worried me even though it was now out of my hands. She promised to ring me in a week even if there was nothing to report.

I left with a heavy heart, knowing I'd done the right thing but possibly gone about it in the wrong way. The police were unhappy when I told them I'd approached Rob Wheeler. It could well be Rob would now lie low for a while and prove problematic to find. In trying to be fair and do the right thing I'd inadvertently warned Rob that the police would be looking for him.

FOURTEEN
SUSAN

Helen Ross, or whatever her name is now, was the last person I expected to see on my doorstep. The last time I saw her, we were both sixteen and barely speaking to each other. No, if I'm honest, it was me who wasn't talking to her, and although I knew how much it must have hurt, I was furious with my one-time best friend for involving me in her troubles. My unfriendly attitude came when Helen most needed me, but we were young and I was scared, particularly when we heard that the man on the bike was dead. My initial fear was of my parents discovering I'd been covering for Helen while she dated Rob and that the police might want to see me if they found out what really happened and that I knew the truth. It was cruel to blank my friend in such a way but she was due to move away, and the time couldn't come soon enough for me and, I suspected, for Helen too.

We'd been friends since primary school, where everyone knew everyone else in our small community. Our parents, however, moved in different circles. My dad was a miner, as was his father before him. Helen's dad was a bank clerk, and a deputy manager, soon to be promoted to manager. They were lovely people and friendly enough when I visited their home, but I still felt they looked down on me, almost as if they were being charitable to their daughter's working-class friend.

Helen was popular at school and I felt special when she chose me as a friend, so I was more than happy to cover for her when she started seeing Rob. I was jealous of her then, too. Rob was attractive with his jet-black hair, dark eyes, and intense stare, which made you feel he could see right into your soul. I blushed almost every time he glanced in my direction, feeling as if he could see every thought as if they were written on my face. Helen didn't cotton on that I was crazy about him, and when she was around, his attention was solely on her. I daydreamed about them splitting up, hoping Rob would then notice me. After all, I was as pretty as Helen and a bit more up to date. Her parents wouldn't let her wear make-up, and her clothes were smart and practical, not the look a teenage girl wanted to present. She'd often come around to my house before a date to put on some make-up, and I'd help her look more fashionable by turning the top of her skirt over a few times to make it shorter or loaning her one of my low-cut trendy tops.

Helen constantly talked about Rob in those early days, telling me everything, which, in a masochistic way, I wanted to hear even though it inflamed my jealousy. The night of the accident was a shock to us both. When Helen arrived on our doorstep, she was trembling and afraid. Her face was swollen where Rob had hit her, and tears stained both cheeks. I might not have believed her story if it wasn't so obvious how upset she was. In some ways, I didn't want to believe it, especially how badly Rob had behaved. Going to the police came into the conversation, and I think I suggested it but I didn't want to get him into trouble; after all, it was an accident. Throughout

Helen's account of the evening, I kept thinking that if she and Rob had fallen out, perhaps he might notice me.

It was only on the following morning that the gravity of the situation fully hit me when the radio reported the cyclist was dead. I was afraid, but for myself, not Helen. If the police found out who'd been driving the car and that I knew all about it but didn't come forward, I'd be some kind of accomplice, wouldn't I? Worse still, if my dad found out, he'd tan me good and proper. My parents weren't refined like Helen's, and Dad wasn't averse to knocking me around a bit to keep me in line.

The only way I could think of to deal with the situation was to distance myself from Helen. It wouldn't be easy, but then I reminded myself how she was deserting me in a few weeks' time anyway when her family moved away. And so, our friendship ended. She quickly got the message that I didn't want to see her anymore and we went our separate ways. For the next few days, I half expected to receive a visit from the police or for them to come into school and drag Helen out in handcuffs. But there was nothing, no big drama or arrest, and as the weeks passed, life returned to normal. Then, Helen's family left Grimethorpe, and our lives moved off in different directions.

Occasionally I've thought about her over the years. We were close for most of our childhood, but I knew I'd never see her again. At that point in my life, I was happy for it to remain so. Once Helen was out of the picture, I set my sights on Rob Wheeler. It didn't bother me he'd knocked down a man; it was an accident which could have happened to anyone, and at last, he noticed me – I was ecstatic. He began hanging around our area again a couple of months after the accident, so I spoke to him to let him know I was on his side. Rob enjoyed attention and I happily pandered to his ego and made him feel important. We quickly became an item and all my dreams seemed to come true.

I couldn't wait to leave school, thinking myself too old to sit in a classroom. I wanted to be out in the world earning money, so I took the first available job at a checkout in the local supermarket. It didn't take long to realise that this life was no better than school, and the only two things which made it bearable were the pay packet each week and knowing Rob and I were still together. Grimethorpe was not a town bursting with opportunity, and although he was trained in motor mechanics, Rob never seemed to find a job which suited him. Still, we rubbed along together without ambition and well-suited to such an undemanding lifestyle.

Within a year of leaving school, I became pregnant. Unsure of Rob's reaction, I kept the news to myself for longer than I should have. But Mum was quick to do her sums and when the morning sickness started, it was impossible to hide the pregnancy any longer in the little terraced house where we lived almost on top of each other. She was more annoyed I hadn't used birth control than that I was sleeping with Rob, and Dad was furious until I plucked up enough courage to remind him how their wedding day was only five months before my birthday. Seventeen was too young to become a mother; we were all in agreement, so I went to the GP to see about an abortion, which had been Rob's first suggestion. The doctor referred me to the hospital, and I waited for a date, somewhat apprehensive about what the abortion would entail. However, I was not to find out.

During the night, severe pain gripped me, the like of which I'd never experienced before, and I started bleeding. The sequence of events afterwards is unclear, but I vaguely recall being in an ambulance with sirens blazing. I remember being prepped for surgery, then nothing more until I woke the following day, hooked up to a drip and feeling incredibly sick and sore. When the doctor eventually came to the ward, he pulled the curtains around my bed, an ominous sign, and told me I'd lost the baby. The news wasn't devastating; after all, I was going to have an abortion, but then he explained how the baby had been growing in the wrong place, an ectopic pregnancy, he called it. If found soon enough, this can be treated, although the baby would not survive. In my case, the foetus developing in the fallopian tubes caused a rupture, hence the incredible pain and the bleeding. The ruptured tube was removed during surgery, but my womb was damaged due to the pressure of a large cyst, so I underwent a hysterectomy. I was young, immature and knowing I couldn't bear children didn't seem too distressing. I knew Rob didn't want a family and thought it wouldn't matter to me either, but over the years, I've often wished we'd had children, a fruitless desire I keep to myself – what's the point of hoping for something which can never be?

Surprisingly, at that particular time, Rob suggested we get married. Prompted by pity or guilt, I neither knew nor cared. We'd intended to live together when we found a house to rent, but the proposal came out of the blue. It was the only time in our relationship when Rob showed any feeling or consideration towards me, although I suspect some of it was in response to pressure from our parents. At the time, I was still so besotted with him and would have been happy for us to be together without being married, yet I jumped at the chance of a wedding before he changed his mind.

It was a small affair at the registry office with only close family and a few friends as guests. Afterwards, there was a buffet at the local pub, nothing fancy, as we could afford very little with hardly any financial help forthcoming from either family. We rented a house just a few streets away from his parents and settled into a routine. I thought I was happy and continued to work at the supermarket, providing our only income, apart from Rob's pittance of dole money, which the landlord at the pub saw more of than I did.

The years passed, perhaps not living up to my girlhood dreams, but I still had Rob and a ring on my finger, which surely meant something. He wasn't a bad husband, a bit free with his fists when he'd had too much to drink, but I quickly learned when to keep out of his way. When he was in one of his dark moods, Rob seemed to need to take it out on someone, if not me, then his brother. I'd witnessed Ricky receiving a couple of vicious beatings for something as trivial as disagreeing with his brother in public.

The supermarket closed down and I lost my job. The whole village was changing as people moved away to find work, their houses left empty, and shops boarded up where once there'd been a thriving community.

A few years ago, Rob unexpectedly appeared to have money and plenty of it. I didn't ask where it came from, assuming a win on the horses or some such windfall, until he told me we were moving to the new estate just a stone's throw from where we were renting. It had to be more than a win on the horses, as the house was amazing, everything new and shining, like something from one of those glossy magazines. Rob gave me money to go shopping too, for new clothes and furniture for the house. I knew better than to question this change in our fortunes and did as he asked, enjoying every minute. We gave up the little terraced rental and moved into our lovely new house, and for the first time in my life, I could have everything I desired, but it came at a price.

My husband had always had an eye for a pretty face, and I was aware of his occasional dalliances yet chose to ignore them. It was always me he came home to, and I still loved him in my own way. And now I could live the life I'd always wanted, financially anyway. New clothes and furnishings became my comfort, as perhaps did food. My weight ballooned with the effect of pushing Rob even further away from me. He still seemed attractive to other women and always having money to splash around enhanced the attraction. But I was his wife even if no longer his lover and settled for the lifestyle my position provided and the attached conditions. Over the last year, Rob was staying away from home more and more frequently, sometimes two or three nights at a time. He offered no explanation and I didn't dare to ask, but around the same time, he seemed to have even more cash than usual and was very generous, which I accepted without question.

Seeing Helen again was nothing short of a shock and stirred old, forgotten feelings. She was well turned out in expensive clothes and was still an attractive woman. I imagined her perfect life, a devoted husband, beautiful children and possibly even grandchildren. Of course, it was all supposition, but the old familiar jealousy wrapped its icy fingers around me again. As girls, I'd often compared myself to her and found myself doing so once again, but this time, I came off worse. Helen's visit unsettled me. My husband almost toyed with her, pretending not to know what she was talking about, but I saw how he looked at her. It had been years since he looked at me in the same way.

Helen's reason for seeking out Rob was a bombshell he didn't take seriously at first. We laughed at the stupidity of wanting to confess to something which happened so long ago, an incident he'd gotten away with, and we didn't for a moment think she would go to the police. But later, as I thought about her unexpected visit, it seemed likely that Helen was serious. She must have put considerable effort into finding out where we lived, and I don't know how far she'd travelled, but again, it was all effort. Rob laughed it off as he did almost everything, refusing to discuss it and heading to the pub, his second and preferred home. Helen gave us two days to respond, and no matter what my husband said, I had a horrible feeling about it all and would be relieved when this *deadline* passed.

FIFTEEN

HELEN

3rd October

The day at Barnsley police station took its toll. I woke the following morning with pain which lasted throughout the day and resorted to an extra dose of painkillers, something I don't like to do, but as Rachel asked, why not? One of the few benefits of knowing you do not have much longer to live is that you no longer have to consider the years ahead, therefore, any long-term damage from the medication is irrelevant.

Megan arrived this morning and asked what kind of day I'd had yesterday while she'd been working. Fudging an answer, I felt uncomfortable, deception generally goes against the grain, but I'm not yet ready to disclose this very worst episode of my life. What would my family think if they knew I'd spent most of the previous day in a police station?

We drank coffee and chatted about Sam and James and the highlights of my daughter's working world. There's always something amusing happening in the surgery and I loved to hear her stories. Megan rolled up her sleeve to reveal scratches which came from a cat who took exception to how the vet attempted to take his temperature. We laughed about it and for a brief moment, the future was forgotten. This is how I wish it could remain, but life rarely works out how we wish. The now constant pain is a reminder of my illness, and for others, well, perhaps they see it in my face. I do try to hide it, but I know whenever my friends or family look at me, primarily, they see a woman who is dying.

Another task I'd set myself to achieve while still able was to sort through the hundreds of family photographs stored in various drawers and boxes. Very few were in albums, so I purchased several with plastic sleeves which held a hundred or more in each volume. These were scattered on the coffee table when Megan arrived, and after coffee, we sorted through them. My daughter always loved looking at photographs, even as a child, but many of these images were of relatives she couldn't remember. I was struck by the importance of giving Megan her history and a sense of belonging.

Photographs today are mostly stored electronically, but there's something more personal about an image you can hold in your hand. I fear generations to come will live their lives vicariously through the screens and devices everyone seems to own, a fear which saddens me. Together we sorted the photos and I carefully wrote names on the back of each one before sliding it into its new plastic sleeve. Megan asked several questions regarding the family connections of some of the more distant and long-gone relatives. After almost two hours of collating the images into albums, my head spun. Yet the task brought a sense of achievement, and our ancestors were suitably displayed and named for future generations. Accomplishing this task brought hope that my grandchildren and their offspring will remember me in years yet to come. With Sam and Ethan being so young, it's hard to know how, or even if, they will remember anything about me, although I'm sure my children will do all they can to preserve their early memories.

After lunch, I slept for an hour and then worried in case I wouldn't sleep at night and ended up scolding myself for being so silly. When you live alone, you no longer have to keep to a routine and I'd fallen into the habit of eating when I was hungry rather than at specific times of the day. The same principle could be applied to sleep, yet I wouldn't wish to become nocturnal. Seeing my family is so important to me, and I shall get back into a routine for their sake and mine, but the previous day had, unsurprisingly, exhausted me.

During the afternoon, I expected a visit from Rachel Amos. Her visits have become precious times to which I look forward. Perhaps because she spends her days with dying people, it's the norm for her and she treats me like a person rather than an invalid. I enjoy her company as I knew I would from the beginning. Rachel is a woman who's not afraid to say what she thinks, something else which others avoid for fear of upsetting me. Not that Rachel does upset me – her realism helps me to be realistic too. I've started jotting down questions which occur between visits to remind me to ask them. Some are medical issues which I prefer to discuss with her rather than my GP, simply because she's a woman. Although my GP and Mr Connors have explained what's happening to my body, Rachel is happy to go over the facts again and clarify anything I don't understand, either because I hadn't taken it in when first told or simply because I've forgotten. She has the knack of simplifying things, using language I can understand, like the stages of cancer. I'm apparently at stage three – the cancer has spread to the lining of the abdomen, the surface of the bowel and the lymph nodes in the pelvis. Pretty rotten luck, isn't it?

Stage four is next, when it will spread to other body parts, such as the spleen and the lungs. By then I'll probably be more than ready to die, and I've come to accept this inevitability and no longer waste time fighting it.

Rachel tells me I'm doing remarkably well for a stage-three patient and is surprised I'm still driving and relatively active. Probably I'm running on sheer stubbornness as I'm determined to make amends for my past and leave things as simple as possible for the children. I can talk to Rachel about my funeral – still a taboo subject with Megan. Having known so many people who've planned their funerals, Rachel has a wealth of knowledge on the topic. I've heard for the first time about eco-friendly coffins woven from fast-growing materials such as willow, sea-grass or bamboo. Presently, I don't think Megan can discuss this, so I want to leave specific instructions to hopefully make the arrangements easier for her and Luke. With Rachel, I can talk about such matters as if discussing the purchase of a bunch of bananas.

At times we've been reduced to tears, laughing at the absurdity of the whole ceremonial aspect of death. I particularly liked one anecdote she shared of a mourner wearing such an obvious toupée. The offending wig slipped out of place and Rachel struggled to maintain her composure throughout the service, her attention drawn to the comical sight. It's not that we ridicule death – Rachel's far too professional for such a thing, but it's a fact of life for which we each have a different coping mechanism and I'd rather adopt the humorous approach. Perhaps I'd feel differently if it was a close relative rather than me who's about to die; who knows? Still, however we approach death, we cannot alter its inevitability, its finality.

Rachel arrived promptly as always, and we drank coffee in the kitchen, watched closely by Gus, hoping for a corner of biscuit for his trouble. I asked about increasing the medication. I'm currently on non-steroidal anti-inflammatory drugs, namely Naprosyn, which seems sufficient most of the time. Occasionally I feel the need for something stronger, mainly to help me sleep. Rachel prescribed painkillers in addition to

Naprosyn, which she suggested I take before bed to see if they helped. I knew the time would come to move on to more potent opioid drugs, but I hoped having to do so would be a few months away yet. My target was to get to Christmas and beyond, although I had no idea if this was a realistic notion, and the doctors were reluctant to predict an actual timeframe. When voicing my hope to Rachel, she nodded enthusiastically, saying having a target was positive. She encouraged me to strive for achievable goals like Christmas and perhaps an event in the new year. I appreciated such a constructive approach, and my respect for this lady grows with every meeting.

Rachel doesn't talk much about herself, not for any secretive reason, but simply because she's a professional and our time together is solely for my benefit. However, she did answer a few of my direct or perhaps nosey questions, and I've learned that she's married to a doctor and has two young daughters. On one visit, I persuaded her to show me the girls' photographs; the elder is her mother's image, with the younger presumably favouring her father. Rachel explained how her mother helped with childcare and I experienced a sudden stab of envy for a woman I'd never met but who was at the centre of her grandchildren's lives. At times like this, I felt most acutely the finality of my approaching death.

These visits never end on a gloomy note. Before Rachel left, we once again found something trivial to laugh about, something I can't relate because it's completely slipped my mind – another little something which is happening more frequently!

Alone again, I lay on the sofa and closed my eyes. Gus jumped up at my feet, and together we slept until awoken by the telephone about an hour later. It was DC Rose Hamilton, whose voice I was not expecting. I probably sounded like I'd just been asleep, which I had.

'It's just a courtesy call, Mrs Reid. We've tried to contact Mr Wheeler a couple of times this week but haven't managed to get hold of him. I wanted you to know we're still working on this but as it's not a priority case and no one is in actual danger, we'll just have to keep trying.' The young police constable sounded pleasant and polite. I knew things wouldn't happen quickly; this might be a major event for me but historic crimes are not at the top of the list of police priorities. I thanked her for calling and keeping me informed, then pulled myself together and took Gus out for a long walk.

SIXTEEN
HELEN

9th October

Having slipped into a routine of staying in bed later than usual, I'm rather cross with myself for doing so. If it weren't for Gus, it would probably be even later, and I don't want to waste my days; they are too precious to fritter away. This morning, however, was a day I could easily have done without. Megan was at work and I wasn't expecting any callers, so I was surprised when the doorbell rang. I certainly didn't feel well enough to play the hostess to anyone; a lazy day at home was all I craved.

Finding DS Greenwood and DC Hamilton on my doorstep was a surprise. As I stepped aside for them to enter, I struggled to understand why they were here without warning, particularly as it was only a few days since DC Hamilton had rung. Tea was offered and declined as the officers sat down and waited for me to do the same. The young woman attempted a smile, clearly forced, and DS Greenwood maintained his professional demeanour with no hint regarding the purpose of their presence here in my living room. He spoke first.

'Mrs Reid, is there anything else you would like to tell us about the incident you reported recently?'

'No, I don't think so.' I was puzzled by the question; surely, they had all the detail they needed.

'Is there anything you'd like to change in your statement of the events of that evening?'

'No, I told you all I could remember. Why, what's happened?' Sudden anxiety knotted my stomach – I needed to know what was happening and looked from the detective to his colleague, who again attempted a smile which was anything but reassuring.

'I'm afraid I'm going to have to ask you to come with us to answer some questions.' DS Greenwood cleared his throat and stood up.

'Where – to the police station?' It was over an hour's journey; we wouldn't get there until lunchtime, and how would I get home? I was upset and confused.

'Are you unwell, Mrs Reid?' The young woman's voice held concern.

'Well, actually, I'm not having a good day. Couldn't you ask your questions here?'

The two officers exchanged a glance. DS Greenwood looked reproachful of his colleague, but she seemed to convey something to him by her look, and he relented.

'Perhaps, under the circumstances...' He sat once more.

'That tea might be nice now, Mrs Reid. Can I help you make it?' The young officer appeared to be going out on a limb and I couldn't help but wonder what it was all about. I led the way into the kitchen and put the kettle on.

'The cups are in the cupboard above the dresser.' I indicated, and she busied herself in getting them out. I wanted to ask questions but felt it prudent to wait until we were settled again with our teacups to study as a distraction. We returned to the lounge, where the DS scrutinised the little group of family photographs I kept on the sideboard. He returned to his chair and took the proffered cup and saucer.

'We managed to speak to Mr Wheeler yesterday and he gave us a somewhat different account of events to your statement.' His eyes held mine, seeking a reaction.

'Well, I'm not surprised. Rob thinks he got away with it – I fully expected him to deny it.' *And*, I was thinking, *surely you should have expected the same.* The DC brought out a notebook and made notes as DS Greenwood maintained eye contact.

'So, will you be doing anything about it?' I asked, not having a clue what would happen next. Would my word be sufficient to bring charges, or would the police think it wasn't worth the effort? And wasn't it the Crown Prosecution Service who decided if a case was strong enough to pursue and if it was in the public interest? Would one person's word be sufficient, or would Rob get away with it all over again? I sipped my tea and waited to be enlightened. The DS took his time before answering.

'Mr Wheeler has presented another version of events which naturally we have to investigate. He claims it was you who was driving the car.' He paused, watching my reaction.

It felt as if I'd been punched in the stomach. I certainly hadn't seen that one coming! My hands trembled and the cup tipped slightly. Rose Hamilton reached over and took the cup from me to place on the coffee table. When I could manage to speak, all I could say was, 'No.'

'Mr Wheeler told us he was giving you driving lessons. He said you'd pleaded with him to do so, despite not having a licence or insurance and being underage.'

I'd been sitting on the edge of the sofa and collapsed into it, unable to speak and feeling physically sick. DC Hamilton moved beside me.

'Do you want some water?' she asked. I shook my head. All I wanted to do was go back to bed and hide beneath the warm duvet with Gus beside me.

'Are you all right, Helen? Can I call someone for you?'

I shook my head again, not wanting anyone to witness this debacle. I'd brought this on myself by trying to put things right – had I only made matters worse? My brain struggled to take in the facts. I knew Rob was lying, but the police didn't, so who would they believe? After a few minutes, I recovered sufficiently to speak.

'So, is it just my word against his?'

'Actually, no. Wheeler's wife has confirmed his story. She claims you visited her after the event and told her everything that happened, including how you were driving. Mrs Wheeler was under the impression you were boasting about it.' The DS scrutinised my face, watching each expression as if trying to decide if I was telling the truth or simply a bitter woman trying, for unknown reasons, to make trouble for Rob Wheeler.

'That's ludicrous! I did go to Susan's but I told her the truth. Rob was driving, not me! Naturally, she'll say it was me now – she's his wife.' By this time tears were rolling down my face. I searched my pocket for a tissue and tried to compose myself.

'Why would I come forward now if I'd been the one driving?' Surely, they could see the logic in that.

'Sometimes people have a desire to be found out but don't possess the courage to admit to what they've done. Accusing someone else is a roundabout way of confessing to something they can't directly face up to.'

It sounded like bizarre psychological reasoning to me, and I wondered if DS Greenwood actually believed it. From the concern in Rose Hamilton's expression, I felt she was more sympathetic than her colleague. The DS continued.

'You must see our dilemma, Mrs Reid, we have one person

telling us one version and two people telling another. We have to take all claims seriously and investigate accordingly.'

'Does this mean you'll be arresting me?' This was scary – what on earth had I got myself into?

'Not at this stage. But I'd like to offer you the chance to revise your statement, and I would caution you to think very seriously about this.'

'There's nothing to change. What I told you was the truth! A man died but I wasn't driving – it was Rob Wheeler. In coming to you to report it I wanted to see justice served and perhaps bring some comfort to the man's family.'

DS Greenwood stood to leave; Rose Hamilton followed.

'What happens now? When will I hear what you're going to do?'

'We'll be in touch in due course. Goodbye, Mrs Reid, thank you for the tea.' The sergeant's face was unreadable. DC Hamilton smiled and nodded as she scurried after him.

'When we know anything new, I'll ring you.' She gently closed the door after her.

They left me feeling so utterly confused. Rose had been the more sympathetic of the two, or was it a case of good cop/bad cop? I collapsed onto the sofa and allowed myself a good old sob. Why had I been so stupid as to drag this up again? It certainly wasn't bringing me the peace I'd hoped and if the police believed Rob and Susan, I might end up being arrested, which was certainly not how I envisaged spending my last few months on earth.

For the rest of the day, I did precisely what I intended not to do – mooch about feeling sorry for myself. What a pathetic individual I am!

SEVENTEEN
SUSAN

I had no choice but to back up Rob's lies to the police – but hey, what's new? Rob makes all the decisions and always has, not only for me but for his mother and brother. My husband insisted Ricky watch the police station in Barnsley for three days to see if Helen carried out her threat of reporting him. As ever, Ricky did his brother's bidding, not daring to stand up to him and tell him to do his own dirty work. But Ricky somehow missed the woman and therefore didn't follow her home as Rob had instructed, and now we don't know where she lives, luckily for her! Yet we do know Helen went to the police as they came to talk to Rob four days after her visit.

My husband proved to be his usual elusive self. He generally managed to be out when anyone called looking for him, particularly the police. If he was at home, I was always sent to answer the doorbell and check out any visitors before admitting Rob was there. He was lucky and managed to avoid the police twice, but knowing they'd find him eventually he decided on an alternative version of the truth.

I must admit Rob can use his brain when needed. He came up with the plausible idea of turning the facts around and telling the police Helen had been driving the car on that long ago, fateful night. He even went to the police station voluntarily to add credence to the story, taking me along to confirm his lies. The look of innocence on his face when the DS told him why they wanted to talk to him almost convinced me it was a surprise. The detective gave only the bones of the facts while Rob sadly nodded, waiting his turn to answer the allegations.

'I'm sorry it's come to this.' He sounded solemn and remorseful. 'It was a night I'll never forget and it was wrong of me not to come forward at the time. I know now. Helen and I had been seeing each other for several weeks, and she'd nagged and pleaded for me to teach her to drive. I knew she was only sixteen, but I suppose I'm not the only man to have given in to a pretty face. It was wrong of me, but the road was quiet, and I certainly didn't expect her to drive so fast. Helen went wild once behind the wheel, laughing and putting her foot down despite my protests.' Rob was well-rehearsed and I almost believed him as he came to the crime.

'We didn't see the man on his bike; he was on a bend in the road which Helen took far too quickly. The poor sod didn't stand a chance. We stopped the car and I could see he was badly injured, if not dead, but Helen became hysterical. She begged me not to go back and I'm sorry to say that I did as she asked in a moment of weakness. I took over the driving, and we left the scene and the injured man. I dropped Helen off near her house, but rather than go home she went to Susan's.' Rob turned to me to confirm and continue his story, which naturally I did, relating Helen's visit on the evening and her *confession* of being the driver of the car. I felt terrible, guilty, but Helen was a stranger to me now and supporting Rob was a given, not an option. I'd learned the hard way over the years that my husband would not be crossed and on the odd occasion I'd differed with him he'd made my life almost unbearable. Rob finished our fictional account by saying he hadn't seen Helen again since the day of the accident, not even admitting to her recent visit, which we were unsure they knew about.

Returning to the car, Rob muttered, 'Good girl' as if I were a pet dog! He must have known I'd play my part. I always do – good old reliable Susan. Standing up to Rob is not a wise choice – he can make life uncomfortable or even painful. My life with him has always been one of doing his bidding and placating him when in one of his dark moods.

Looking back on my life objectively, it seems weird to have been content with the way things are. Generally, we've rubbed along together without any real happiness and very little affection. Seeing Helen again has in some way introduced a seed of restlessness into my life. Apathy has been my constant companion over the years, and I'd drifted along wasting time and energy in a totally useless life, which I am now beginning to regret.

As girls, Helen and I had much in common. We were both pretty, reasonably intelligent, doing well at school and with the whole world at our feet. When Helen moved away, we were both glad, but for very different reasons. It appears my friend went on to make something of her life, whereas I settled into a dreary complacency. Whether this was the result of remaining in Grimethorpe or because I settled for Rob as a life partner, I don't know. Helen and I have so obviously led very different lives. Perhaps I'm assuming hers was better than mine, an assumption based on only one recent meeting, but the old jealousy has returned to unsettle me and being the one who ended up as Rob's wife no longer seemed the prize it once did.

So, what will happen next? I have no idea. Hopefully, the police will believe Rob's version of events, particularly with me to back him up, but what about Helen? She doesn't deserve to be blamed for this. I know it in my heart, but Rob is my husband

– my loyalty has to be to him. Besides, I would never dare cross him. Perhaps the police will decide that the case doesn't merit further investigation – it was so long ago, and with no solid evidence how can they continue?

Rob isn't entirely unknown to the police. There've been a few occasions when he's narrowly avoided trouble with the law over petty incidents – black market cigarettes and counterfeit DVDs, but would it go against him now? I was also anxious in case the police came to the house.

Rob keeps a gun in his wardrobe and I know he doesn't have a licence. He also doesn't know I've seen it. It was a disturbing find and although shocked I didn't dare ask him about it. Since then, I've wondered why he should need a gun. It's a small handgun, not that I know anything about firearms, but it's heavy and I think it's loaded. There's a box of bullets too. The presence of a gun in my home is uncomfortable, but it's something I need to keep to myself. I wonder if Rob's ever used it or if he would. It suggested that my husband was into crime at a higher level than I thought, but if I'm honest I knew the large amounts of cash must come from illegal activities. Rob quite freely splashes it around and, over the years, has given me considerable amounts, no doubt to keep me from asking questions. Does that make me an accomplice?

Over the next few days, I frequently thought about Helen. If I were her, I'd be sorry to have opened up such a can of worms, and I honestly can't think of any reason why she would. We didn't know her married name, which for her was a blessing. If Rob found out her full name and where she lived, he'd probably have paid her an unpleasant and intimidating visit before she managed to report to the police.

In my mind, Helen has achieved everything I have not. She's kept her girlish figure, evident in her well-cut, quality clothes. Her hair is immaculately styled with no grey showing through, unlike mine, which needs colouring every couple of weeks. Her presence in my home made me feel decidedly uncomfortable. Perhaps Helen also seemed awkward but maintained a poised demeanour, despite not getting what she came for. I honestly don't know why she's dragging this up so long after it happened. Surely she'd have tried to forget the incident. I've rarely thought about it, and I'm pretty sure Rob had forgotten it, too, until Helen turned up out of the blue.

We dutifully went back to the police station the following day to make formal statements, which were videoed, and Rob once again briefed me on precisely what to say, in which as usual I had no choice.

EIGHTEEN
HELEN

10th October

The only positive in my mind today is that it surely can't be worse than yesterday. I slept poorly last night, but it wasn't the pain keeping me awake this time but my mind, tumbling with thoughts about the past and uncertainties of the future. In my clumsy attempt to sort this incident out and make recompense, albeit late, I'd made things worse. This was not how I wanted my family to learn about my past mistakes, and they certainly will if I'm arrested.

In my fitful dreams, handcuffs which chafed at my wrists constrained me and weighed heavily, physically and mentally. I awoke early, knowing there would be no more sleep, and went downstairs, followed by an expectant Gus. The poor dog would have to make do with a sniff around the garden instead of his usual lengthy walk; I was tired, with a headache and a raging thirst. After letting him into the garden, I drank two glasses of water and set the kettle to boil for tea. My mind was a fog of jumbled thoughts; it was not the perfect time to make decisions, but it was imperative to have a plan from which to work.

I thought about ringing the police station and asking to speak to DC Rose Hamilton. She was certainly more sympathetic than her colleague, but what would have changed in less than twenty-four hours? No, I'd have to wait – something which irritated me now more than it used to, but in my former life, I had all the time in the world. This was no longer the case. Hearing Gus scratching at the kitchen door, I let him in and treated him to a few cornflakes with milk. It was still dark outside. I wanted to ring Megan, but it was too early; their household wouldn't be stirring for another hour at least. After making tea and putting bread into the toaster, I again reached for the painkillers, taking twice as many as I should in the hope they would relieve not only the physical pain but the mental anguish I'd brought upon myself.

I must have dozed off on the sofa, for daylight streamed through the windows when I awoke, and my tea and toast were cold, untouched on the coffee table in front of me. The headache had eased somewhat and I checked the time; twelve o'clock. I'd been asleep for over four hours. Nibbling on the cold toast, I wondered what to do next. By now, Megan would be at work, too late to ring her, but it was perhaps a good time to speak to Luke in Canada. I booted up the laptop and clicked on Skype. Within seconds Imogen's face appeared on the screen. I smiled at my daughter-in-law, who beamed back at me with such enthusiasm I could have cried.

Before saying much more than hello, Ethan's face popped up in front of his mother, and a stream of excited chatter began. I listened to his semi-coherent monologue, blinked back the tears and smiled at this delightful little boy who was part of me, an incredible thought! It was good to know something of their life in Canada, and as Ethan chattered away about the beach, I had a mental image of the two of us skimming stones into the water. Imogen sat back and allowed her son to steer the conversation, prompting him occasionally on incidents she thought I might like to hear.

After ten minutes, Imogen's attention was distracted as Luke appeared. I almost felt part of their domestic scene as Ethan ran towards his daddy, and Imogen turned the screen so I could see him hugging Luke's legs, a massive grin on his little face. Of course, we'd spoken many times lately, but today my need for family comfort was heightened by recent events. As Ethan ran out of news to share, he went off to play, and Luke took over at the screen, asking firstly about my health. I answered as honestly as I could, playing down the bad days to avoid worrying him and trying desperately to think of something positive to say. Rachel Amos popped into my mind, so I told him how much her visits were helping and what an excellent source of information she was. I then deliberately changed the subject to ask about Luke's job and listened to how much he enjoyed the work and their lifestyle in Canada.

'Actually, Mum, we were going to Skype you tonight.' His grin made me curious.

'Go on then, tell me!'

'I've booked a flight to the UK. We're coming over for Christmas!'

Tears escaped then, but tears of joy rather than the *feeling sorry for myself* tears of earlier. I couldn't have received better news; both my children would be here for Christmas. How wonderful! Luke had mulled over the idea of coming over himself, but for them all to come was marvellous. After a few more minutes, we said our goodbyes, and I immediately texted Megan to share the good news. Only after did I realise I was still in my dressing gown and had done absolutely nothing constructive all morning. A quick shower was in order, and suddenly I felt so much better than earlier – due to the extra painkillers or the good news from Luke, I didn't care as I went quickly back upstairs to make myself feel human again.

Showered and dressed, I finally took Gus for his much-needed walk, feeling lighter than I had for the last couple of days. Gus seemed to sense the mood and ran to and fro, bringing sticks for me to throw and barking playfully as I gave him the attention he craved. My mood had shifted, propelled by good news rather than only the bad which dominated my life at present but which I had, admittedly, brought upon myself.

It was already October and I knew Christmas would be upon us soon, so I needed to plan and prepare. Not knowing how I'd be feeling by December spurred me on, presenting a goal to work towards with no time to waste.

11th October

I spent the rest of yesterday making plans, my mood buoyed by the news that Luke, Imogen and Ethan would be here for Christmas. This morning, I've been thinking more about the bucket list I'd wanted to make and some of the ideas I'd mentally considered when I began writing this journal. Yes, the trip to Canada had been the one big highlight, a very positive experience and one I could remember with joy as I thought of the wonderful time spent there.

But the other *big* thing on the list was the not-so-good memory and my burning desire to make amends for the most horrendous experience from my youth. It would certainly be accurate to say this is the item from the bucket list which has almost consumed my life, bringing pain and confusion with, as yet, no closure on the issue at all. Having taken the irrevocable step of involving the police, I now wondered if I could find a different way of dealing with it. The police moved slowly in historic cases, I knew and understood this, but I feared there would be insufficient time for me to see this through to the end, and I didn't want to die without the matter being resolved one way or another.

I was toying with the idea of approaching Susan Wheeler and appealing to her good nature. (Surely there was still some of the goodness in her that I'd known as a child.) But how to manage this was another problem. It would necessitate another trip to Grimethorpe, not something which appealed to me in the least, but even then, there'd be the problem of trying to see her without alerting Rob. I needed to apply more thought to the idea rather than blunder into it and perhaps make matters even worse.

And what about some of the more positive plans on my bucket list? I'd almost completed the organisation of our family photographs, no outstanding achievement there, but something practical which pleased me in the happy memories those images recorded.

If truth be told, I possessed no burning desire to do anything spectacular. Never one to be adventurous or sporty, a parachute jump or wing walking wasn't something I wished to consider, and I'm certainly past doing any other strenuous activity. Had Andrew been alive it would have been so different, not the risky activities but other more positive ideas. We loved to travel and had grand plans for our retirement. But having travelled to Canada alone, I knew there would be no more long-distance trips. Yet I'd had a wonderful time, and often recall meeting Tim, a strange bittersweet experience but an encounter I was glad to have experienced.

As my world has now shrunk into the parameters of what I can do physically, so too has my bucket list, but there are still things to anticipate with pleasure. One of these is celebrating Megan's birthday next week by taking her out for a day –

perhaps for a nice meal and some shopping in Leeds or Manchester. My children have never had expectations of what we should do as parents, and Megan always puts other people before herself. Of course, it's also Luke's birthday and even as children, my daughter gave in to what her brother wanted to do to celebrate. As an adult, she still tries to please everyone and generally cooks a family meal to celebrate birthdays together, even her own. We could go on the train, which would be much easier and less stressful than finding convenient parking, and take a taxi back to the station if we wanted. Yes, a *girlie* day, don't they call it these days? I would love to spoil Megan, and hopefully, she won't protest too much. I'll make a point of fixing a date with her soon.

Now Luke will be here for Christmas, I can plan for that too and perhaps choose presents with Megan's help. I can also add baking to my list; the sooner I prepare for Christmas, the better. It wasn't yet decided where Luke would stay, but I have so much more room than Megan, so here seems the obvious choice. I'd enjoy making all his favourite cakes and dishes in advance and freezing them until they were needed.

Looking at the garden today also prompted something else I must do, namely to find a gardener to tackle the outside work before winter takes over completely. Andrew was the family gardener, I'm very much a fair-weather potterer, but even I can see how much the trees and shrubs need pruning, a task well beyond my present capabilities. And now another thing on the to-do list is to give more thought to contacting Susan Wheeler.

Compared to my emotional state after DS Greenwood's visit, I'm somewhat improved and much more positive. The pain medication seems to be kicking in too, which is a huge plus as the pain affects how I feel emotionally as well as physically. A degree of my usual motivation appears to have returned, so I must take advantage of it while it lasts.

12th October

I was Rachel's first patient this morning and was up waiting, with the kettle boiled and a dozen things to tell her. She smiled at my apparent good mood, and after initial inquiries about how I was and whether the increased medication was working, I almost bombarded the poor girl with all my news. However, she seemed genuinely pleased and interested when I told her of Luke's forthcoming visit and my plans to shop and prepare for Christmas while I felt able to do so.

Rachel's a very 'together' young woman in the sense that nothing appears to surprise her – she copes with everything thrown at her in a relaxed, cool manner. This doesn't mean she's unfriendly – quite the opposite. Perhaps unflappable or calm would be a better way to describe her. Rachel is good to have around during bad times – well-informed in her professional role, she imparts her wisdom intelligently yet straightforwardly, precisely what I need.

My nurse appeared to have more time than usual this morning. Although she never rushes our visits, I'm always conscious that there are other patients for her to see, and her working life is busy. At one point, I almost shared my situation regarding Rob Wheeler and how my plan seemed to be backfiring on me. I didn't, however, as it's not directly related to cancer and an issue she can do nothing about, even though it would be good to have someone in whom to confide. But the moment passed, and I tried to put the whole sorry mess from my mind, not crossing bridges and all that.

NINETEEN
HELEN

13th October

Naturally, Megan was every bit as thrilled as me about Luke's visit, and as we sat on the train heading for Manchester, we chattered like schoolgirls about our plans for Christmas. I maintained there was more space at my house and they should stay with me, while my daughter worried it might be too much as, admittedly, we didn't know quite how I would be by then. We compromised by deciding they could sleep at my house, but we would all eat together at hers. Still wishing to contribute towards the meals, I would hopefully have my freezer stocked with all kinds of Christmas goodies well before the day arrived.

The journey was relatively short, with sufficient time to have a coffee while we discussed our plans, and all too soon, we arrived at Manchester. My attention then focused on Megan, whose birthday was only a couple of days away. I intended to treat her to something expensive and indulgent and ignore all protests. Having never been materialistic, Megan had become adept at living on a budget at university, finding fantastic bargains in the local charity shops. I knew my daughter would baulk at any extravagance, but I had an idea of something she would love and about six hours to work on her.

The distance to the shops wasn't far, but we took a taxi into the heart of the city to conserve our energy for the serious business of shopping. It was midweek, relatively quiet in the shops and somewhat early for the Christmas shoppers, so the perfect time to have chosen. Browsing at the handbag display in the first shop we entered, I picked up one or two to examine more closely. I lifted a beautiful leather one which any woman would love, but Megan frowned at the price ticket, took it from my hands and replaced it on the display. I laughed as we moved on, but wouldn't be put off by my daughter's guilt at owning something extravagant. After covering almost every inch of one department store, we stopped for coffee, both ready to sit down. Megan bought the coffee, and when we were seated, I told her I wanted to buy her a leather jacket, a good one which would last for years. Her face was a picture of surprise; she hadn't expected this, and I smiled at her wide-eyed reaction. As her protest began, I stopped her.

'Megan, everything I have will come to you and Luke soon. So please let me spoil you for this last birthday I'll share with you. It will bring me as much pleasure as it will you.'

Her eyes filled with tears; I knew thinking about the future, or rather the lack of a future with me, was still painful for her. But she could hardly refuse and we headed out of the store to a leather shop I'd discovered while searching the internet.

The wonderful smell of the leather goods enveloped us as we entered the store, a narrow but very long shop which must have stocked hundreds of leather coats and jackets. I instructed Megan to look at them but not at the price tickets. I need not have worried – no price tickets were displayed, a sure sign of how expensive they were! We spent the best part of an hour looking around, and Megan tried on dozens of jackets before narrowing her choice down to two or three. Eventually, she selected a soft leather and suede combination with a 'waterfall' front which fell gently from the shoulders. It was shaped at the waist and very flattering, although her figure was perfect anyway. I could tell how much she liked the jacket by how she hugged it to her, turning in front of the mirror to see it from different angles, eyes sparkling with pleasure.

I sent Megan to look at the accessories at the far end of the shop while I completed the transaction with a delighted shopkeeper; there was no reason for my daughter to know the price. When I joined her at the far end of the shop, we looked at handbags, purses and wallets. I wanted to choose something James might like for Christmas and a gift for Luke too. We decided on a smart leather briefcase for James, my daughter only protesting slightly, and a beautiful wallet and leather iPad cover for Luke. We also bought a gorgeous soft leather handbag for Imogen. I was so enjoying myself – the personification of a woman spending as if there was no tomorrow!

After over an hour, we left the shop with two large bags, carried by Megan, and headed for the toy shop. Sam and Ethan would have been in heaven – there were so many lovely toys and games I didn't know where to start. We decided on a basic model railway with track, engine and carriages for Sam, something he could add to as he got older, and a massive box of Lego for Ethan. I wanted to buy them there and then but carrying such bulky purchases would be problematic, particularly as I was strictly forbidden by my daughter to carry anything at all. The answer was to confine ourselves to window shopping and make a list to order on the internet at home; there was still plenty of time until Christmas.

Lunch was next on the agenda and we stumbled upon a lovely patisserie with a tempting display in the window and a mouth-watering menu of paninis, salads and soup. Finding a table beside the window, we ordered more than I could eat. The patisserie was quiet, so we were under no pressure to leave. We ate slowly and ordered a second pot of tea, enjoying the food and the relaxing atmosphere.

It was difficult not to talk about what was constantly on my mind and the practical issues my impending death presented. Still, I restrained myself from reeling off a list of things I wanted Megan to do after I was gone (or D-Day, as I now thought of it). Instead, I kept the conversation light for my daughter's sake – concentrating on happier things, namely Luke's visit. This common ground served us well in keeping the atmosphere light and was something we were both excited about.

After a leisurely lunch, tiredness descended and we returned to the station. The only condition I made to going home so soon was that we went through the first store we'd visited. Once inside, I bought Megan the lovely leather bag we'd seen earlier, it was a perfect match for the jacket, and I waved away her protestations – there was no need to remind her I'd not be around for her next birthday.

Once home, after letting Gus into the garden, I lay on the sofa and fell instantly asleep. It had been a good, productive day and another tick could be added to the bucket list alongside *spoiling Megan*. However, I still fully intended to spoil all my family at every opportunity.

14th October

The following morning, I awoke with a throbbing headache, feeling like someone was hammering inside my brain. On standing up, I had to dash to the bathroom, where I was violently sick. This had occurred a couple of times recently, unpleasant episodes which could also lessen the effect of my medication. Rachel advised that if such an episode came within an hour of taking medication, I should repeat the dose. This morning, however, I'd had nothing and waited an hour or so until I could eat a slice of toast and take the medication. I suppose I'll have to get used to such symptoms and live my life around them.

The plan for today was to visit my mother at the care home. By ten o'clock, I was sufficiently recovered to drive and set off to The Valley, about twenty minutes' drive from home. After signing in, I went in search of Mum, finding her in her room. After kissing her forehead, I launched into the customary one-sided conversation which was sadly the norm. I put the cheerful yellow chrysanthemums I'd brought in a vase and topped it up from the sink in the bathroom. When I placed them on the windowsill, Mum suddenly reached out and knocked them over. A torrent of abuse commenced with such awful language and I was almost frozen to the spot. I'd never before heard such words used by my usually genteel, softly-spoken mother. A nurse appeared in the doorway, alerted by the commotion and once again, Mum needed to be sedated. Finding myself in the matron's office, I was upset at what was happening. Knowing acting out of character is often displayed in people with Alzheimer's, I feared that Mum would have to be moved to another home, one designed to cope with such issues. The matron, however, reassured me this would only be a last resort. There were other initiatives to try first, including different medication. She also told me they'd found the owner of the jewellery which was secreted away in Mum's room. It belonged to another resident whom the staff believed had given the items to my mother, which was such a relief to know. I didn't want to think she'd turned into a jewel thief.

'You know, it's rather like looking after children,' the matron told me, 'and we don't think any the less of your mother whatever she does or says. It's the disease which makes her act out of character, and I constantly hear about residents who have been delightful people until Alzheimer's took its hold, so please don't worry. I'm sure we can work around these problems and her GP is coming this afternoon if you'd like to be here?'

The answer would generally have been yes, but I didn't feel up to returning for the second time in a day. The matron understood, aware of my health issues which I told her about some time ago, knowing she needed to know what was happening on the family front. Besides, I had every confidence in the GP, who had been our family doctor for several years.

Once home again, I rang Megan to update her on her grandmother's condition. We laughed about me thinking she'd turned into a jewel thief – sometimes, laughter's the only way to cope. We recalled some of the strange things Mum had done, particularly in the early stages of her illness when we just put it down to old age. There was the time she insisted she'd been robbed when her slippers had disappeared. We tried to tell her that a burglar would have taken other items of more value than a tatty pair of slippers, but my favourite story is when she went to a new hairdresser and as they took her to the back-wash sink to shampoo her hair, Mum knelt up on the seat and put her head in forwards. Then one time she bought a new washing machine and kept calling it a Suzuki rather than a Zanussi. Laughter is by far a much better option than crying about such things.

The matron rang later in the afternoon. The doctor had taken blood samples and altered Mum's medication slightly. He would visit again in a few days to see if things were any better. Again, I thanked her, expressing my appreciation and admiration for all the staff who did such a stellar job, which certainly not easy.

Megan will need no prompting to take care of my mother as she visits her grandmother almost as often as I do, alleviating one of the concerns I still harbour. Mum rarely recognises me these days, but she's still a huge part of my life.

16th October

Yesterday was Megan's birthday. I could see on her face that she was trying to be strong while inevitably thinking about next year when I wouldn't be around. We went to our favourite restaurant for a lovely meal in the evening, just Megan, James, Sam and me. Megan wore her new jacket and looked stunning. Her blonde curls had been brushed until they shone, and her blue eyes were wide and sparkling. After eating far too much, we went back home to Skype Luke, who was also celebrating his birthday. It was nine in the evening here, but for them, it would be four in the afternoon, and I knew they'd be at home, waiting for our call. With four of us crowding around our end of the computer and Luke's family the same in Canada, Megan and James made an announcement.

'We're going to have a baby!'

I was genuinely pleased to hear such wonderful words, but it also struck a cruel blow to my heart, knowing I'd not be around to see this new grandchild.

When the call to Luke ended, Megan went into the kitchen to make coffee while James took a sleepy Sam upstairs to get ready for bed. Following into the kitchen, I put my arm around my daughter's shoulder.

'I'm so thrilled about your news. I know how much you've both longed for another child.'

Megan turned towards me, tears in her eyes. Perhaps only then did I fully understand the meaning of the word *bittersweet*.

'I've wanted to tell you for ages, Mum, but didn't know how...' She rested her head on my shoulder and cried softly as I stroked her hair, making those universal *shh* noises to calm and comfort my girl. After a few moments, Megan lifted her head and looked at me.

'I'm sorry, Mum, I should have known you'd be pleased for us, but I thought it might be too much – you know? It seems like giving you a precious gift and then taking it away again.'

'Yes, love, I understand, but we can enjoy this pregnancy together, can't we?'

'Of course, and I have an appointment for a scan next week. Will you come with me?'

There was no need to answer. I was so grateful that Megan wanted me with her. They didn't have scans when the twins were born, and James accompanied her during her first pregnancy, so this was very new and exciting for me, and I could hardly wait.

TWENTY

HELEN

17th October

I finally reached a decision last night. Having slept badly,
even with extra painkillers, I spent half the night thinking about
Megan and the delightful news of her pregnancy and the other
half worrying over my position regarding Rob and Susan's lies.
Then, as I tossed and turned in the inky silence of my bedroom
with only the tick of the alarm clock and the even breathing of
Gus for company, I decided to visit Susan. What I would say to
her I wasn't sure. Appealing to her better nature could prove
difficult. Did she even have one, especially after being married
to Rob for all these years? But I was going, and that very
morning too.

Anticipating the problem of finding Susan alone, I decided
it was simply a risk I'd have to take. Rob could be out at work if
he had a job to go to, of course. One option with which I'd
wrestled in the small hours of the morning was to write Susan a
letter. The danger was that Rob might open it – I could see him
being the controlling sort. The compromise I eventually reached
was to write a letter to take with me and if Rob was in, attempt
to give Susan the letter on the quiet. It seemed feasible at three

forty this morning, but I wasn't as certain later as I took out my pad and paper to write. Still, it was better to do something other than wait around and worry about what might happen, and it was such a terrible situation which surely couldn't get any worse.

Attempting to keep awake as I drove, I turned the volume of the CD player high and listened to the haunting music from *The Phantom of the Opera*. I'd have sung along with gusto at one time, but not this morning. Pain gripped my body, its burning tendrils worming under my skin. I couldn't say exactly which part as everywhere hurt, even my brain, which struggled against my resolve to drive to Grimethorpe. The sky was grey, heavy with storm clouds, somewhat appropriate for the day's task. I could feel the wind tugging at the steering wheel and clenched it tightly until my knuckles hurt too.

Arriving at lunchtime, I parked at the end of the cul-de-sac with a view of Rob's house, or at least part of it. There was no car in the drive, hopefully a good sign, although it could be in the garage. Sitting there trying to muster courage didn't work, so I exited the car and walked determinedly up to the house, forcing myself to raise my arm and ring the doorbell when what I really wanted to do was to turn around and go home. Susan answered within seconds, her face contorting to a scowl when she saw me.

'What do you want?' There were to be no pleasantries.

'Just to talk. Is Rob home?'

'No, but he sure as hell wouldn't want to talk to you if he was.'

'Actually, it was you I came to see.' I tried to keep my voice pleasant, non-confrontational.

Susan looked me up and down, then stood aside to allow me in. It was such a relief knowing Rob wasn't there, but my one-time friend's continued scowl told me she wouldn't make this visit easy. I followed her into the lounge and sat down even though not invited. Susan remained silent, waiting for me to state my purpose.

'The police visited me,' I blurted out, 'and told me what you and Rob had said.' Her expression didn't alter. *Poker face.*

'I know it's a lie, and you and Rob know it too, so why? I know he's your husband, but to lie for him and deliberately blame me, why, Susan?'

No answer was forthcoming, but she turned away from my gaze to look out of the window. Could she have a conscience after all?

'We were friends once, close friends, do you remember? We often wished we were sisters and planned to be friends forever, be each other's bridesmaids, and push prams together when our children arrived. Friends forever, Susan, does it not mean anything to you?'

She turned back to glower at me.

'Cut the sentimental rubbish, won't you? We'll never be friends again – you know that as much as I do!'

'But we can at least be civil to each other. We're adults now, and the world has enough sorrow and bitterness without causing more.'

'Oh, you want to save the world now, do you?' Her words were liberally laced with sarcasm. 'Grow up, Helen, this isn't going to happen and the more you push us, the worse things will be for you. Rob isn't a patient man and can make life pretty difficult for you if he's so inclined. My advice would be to go home, wherever it is, and stay out of his way.'

'I can't – now I've been to the police, they have to do something. They won't drop this even if I go back to tell them I've changed my mind – they have to investigate to find the truth.'

'But why do it at all? It was years ago – okay, the man died, but dragging it all up again won't bring him back, and his wife's probably married someone else by now and won't want to be reminded of it.' She was genuinely puzzled; perhaps I owed her the truth.

'I'm ill, Susan. I have cancer and it's not treatable. I don't expect you to understand, but I must put this right before my time runs out. It's always been there, in the back of my mind, and not having done the right thing then, I'm trying to do it now.'

My one-time friend stared at me, incredulous.

'Is it true? You're not just playing the sympathy card, are you?'

'It's true.'

Susan pulled her bulky frame out of the chair. 'Come through to the kitchen,' she said.

I obeyed the order, following her into a huge kitchen where she moved around, setting the kettle to boil and reaching for cups from the cupboard. I sat on a stool next to the peninsular which divided the kitchen from a dining area, watching. Neither of us spoke – perhaps she was wondering what to say, just as I was. The kitchen was equipped with every modern convenience imaginable. A juicer and an ice-cream maker stood on the gleaming work surfaces, and the usual toaster, kettle and microwave, all in pristine condition as if they'd never been used. Susan made coffee and put the welcome cup of hot liquid in front of me before taking the stool opposite.

'You don't take sugar, do you?' It was a statement as much as a question and it gave me hope. She did remember our long-ago friendship. I smiled and thanked her for the coffee.

'How long – I mean, how bad is it – the cancer?' Her face held a softer expression and I could see a little of the old Susan still there.

'It's difficult to know. I hope to be reasonably well over

Christmas, and then it's a matter of waiting to see what the new year brings. Two or three months, four if I'm lucky.'

'Lucky! Hell, it must be awful for you. I can't imagine knowing I was going to die. Can't they give you chemotherapy or something?'

'No, it's too late, but we all must go sometime.' The old chestnut came out again.

'Yes, but you're not even sixty yet. Next summer's your birthday. What about your family? Husband, children, it must be difficult for them?' She did remember!

'My husband died three years ago. I have two children, twins, a boy and a girl, and yes, it is hard on them. What about you, any children?'

'No. I got pregnant once, but there were complications and I lost it. I needed a hysterectomy afterwards, so there was no chance of any children for me – just as well I suppose, Rob never wanted a family.'

Rob, again, everything revolved around that self-centred bloody man!

'You have a lovely home. Rob must have a good job. Did he stick with mechanics?' It was somewhat surreal chatting over coffee like this. Susan laughed.

'Him, work, that's a good one! Let's say he invests, buying and selling, that kind of thing. I don't ask questions which suits us both. I don't want to know where the money comes from.'

'It's strange for his mother to still live in Straight Street when Rob's doing so well.'

'Ah yes, his sainted mother! She'll never leave the old place until they carry her out in a box. Stubborn as a mule she is, but I don't mind – he wanted her to move in with us, heaven forbid! Then there's his gormless brother, Ricky – not the full shilling, but happy to do his brother's bidding. He gets paid well enough for his trouble but has a liking for the horses. He could have bought a stableful with what he's lost on them.' Susan appeared more relaxed, almost friendly. Whether telling her about the cancer softened her a little or made me seem less of a threat, I don't know, but we'd established a rapport of sorts and my only problem was how to use it to my advantage.

'And your parents, are they still around?'

'Mum is, but Dad died ten years ago. She's in a home now in Barnsley, so I don't get to visit much, and yours?'

'Almost the same, actually. Dad died a few years ago, and Mum's in a care home for people with dementia. I visit, but she rarely knows who I am.' There was a brief silence as we both pondered the similarities of our lives while aware of the vast differences. I wondered if I should get to the point of my visit or perhaps let the conversation roll on. I decided on the latter.

'Did you ever think of leaving Grimethorpe? It's changed, so many homes and shops are boarded up. It was never a thriving town but there's no heart left here now.'

'Tell me about it! I'd have been happy to leave, move to Sheffield or Leeds perhaps, but Rob likes Grimethorpe. He does most of his business in Leeds but prefers to live here. It makes him feel important, you know, a big fish in a small pond. It drives me mad sometimes, but I like the house and can always go to the city to shop if I want to.'

Although nothing was said directly, I sensed Susan lived a lonely life. A beautiful house doesn't compensate for friends and family.

'Is there anyone you still see from school?' I asked, trying to keep the conversation light.

'No, they've all gone, moved away and I can't say I blame them. More coffee?'

This was weird – as if we were old friends catching up over coffee when a colossal lie was hanging over us, a lie I desperately wanted Susan to disown.

'No, but thank you, I was ready for that. Susan, you must realise I've come to ask you to tell the police the truth?' The scowl reappeared and she turned away.

'I know being Rob's wife puts you in a difficult position, but you know he was driving, not me. So please, I'm only asking you to tell the truth?' She was shaking her head quite emphatically.

'No, there's no way it's going to happen! Rob would kill me – he's got a vile temper. You don't know what he's capable of!'

Perhaps I didn't know, but I could guess. Susan's face reflected a genuine fear. Outwardly things might appear harmonious but her reactions told me otherwise.

'Does Rob hit you, Susan?' The question came out before I'd properly thought it through. The man had a history of violence, even all those years ago when I'd known him. I vividly remember the night of the accident when he hit me with such force. I could almost still see the hatred and anger contorting his face. Susan didn't answer, although her body language gave her away. She almost shrank back and could no longer meet my eyes. Her face flushed and she chewed at the thumbnail on her right hand.

'If you support him in this lie and it goes to court, you'll be guilty of perjury. You know, don't you, Susan?' It was a big thing I was asking of her, but could her silence mean she was considering it? 'I could take you to the police station. They'll understand if you tell them now and probably not press any charges. It's the right thing to do.'

'Right for who?' Susan sounded angry, close to tears. 'Rob isn't someone to cross, Helen. I've seen what he can do. You don't know what you're asking of me!'

I nodded, deciding I'd pushed her far enough. Perhaps with time to think, she'd change her mind. If I tried too much, it would only put distance between us where some progress had been made. A tentative bond was developing, partly from our history of friendship as girls or maybe because Susan was lonely and needed a friend.

I left, telling her she could call me on the number I'd previously given them. I'd kept the phone; it was back in the drawer where I'd found it.

'I don't have it. Rob tore it up.' It was good she told me this, Susan was in effect asking for the number, so I quickly wrote it out again, thanked her for listening and for the coffee, and left.

The drive home gave me time to consider the meeting with Susan. It had gone better than expected, particularly after I told her about the cancer. But apparently I'd failed in my quest to persuade her to tell the truth. Naturally, she was frightened of Rob and with good reason but to what degree it wasn't easy to judge. I wondered what he was into and how he made his money. She'd let slip that he didn't have a job, but the money to fund their lifestyle came from somewhere. The house and furnishings were not cheap, and Susan didn't work, so Rob was somehow making money under the radar. He wasn't the type to be into serious organised crime, or at least I didn't think so unless he was working for someone who was. Still living in Grimethorpe didn't appear to fit either if Rob was into big-time crime, but then as Susan said, he preferred being a big fish in a small pond. In Grimethorpe, he was at the top of the ladder – he'd be just another small-time criminal in the city. Or could it be that Grimethorpe was the perfect place to hide, to keep a low profile? But then again, it could simply be me reading too many detective stories in the middle of the night when I can't sleep. It's amazing what the imagination can conjure up; with just a snippet of information, a whole story can evolve, but could any of my speculation be more than pure fiction?

TWENTY-ONE
HELEN

1st November

The last few days have been a blessing, if only for the peace and quiet they have afforded. My body welcomed the rest, and the pain lessened somewhat from the previous days of pushing myself into almost constant activity.

For now, there was nothing more I could do regarding Susan, Rob and the police. It was a waiting game, which isn't easy when you know your time is limited. So, I tried to rest and catch up on some reading to distract my thoughts from the uncertainties cluttering my mind. Today would most certainly be a good one as I was to accompany Megan to the hospital to see the first images of the baby, the closest I'd get to meeting my newest grandchild.

We drove into an unusually quiet hospital car park and found a space close to the main building. It was a relief to be entering the hospital for a reason other than to have my condition monitored, and a much happier reason, too. The X-ray department was off the main corridor, where we waited our turn in a bright, spacious room with one or two other pregnant women and a handful of patients waiting for general X-rays.

As we sat, watching the activity around us, I saw the unmistakable red hair of Rachel Amos pass by the doorway. She stopped, took a step backwards, and, on recognising me, came into the room smiling broadly. It was an excellent opportunity to introduce her to my daughter, who'd often heard me speak of Rachel and how much her visits helped me. Rachel congratulated Megan and asked the usual questions about dates and so forth before their conversation moved on to compare notes on their other children.

I watched those two young women chattering about their respective families, and I admit to experiencing a stab of envy as they both had so much life still to live and enjoy. It wasn't that I begrudged either of them their futures, but perhaps the feeling came from the realisation of how time passes so swiftly, something we rarely think of when we're young, yet something we're powerless to alter. I felt a sudden urge to tell them both to live each moment to the full, to enjoy their children and make every day count, for we will never have today to live again. Once the sun goes down, the day is lost forever. I resisted the urge to preach this little homily to them, not wanting to present them with the confirmation that I was quickly becoming a batty old woman.

Rachel left us, and Megan's name was very soon called for the scan. In the small examination room, she hoisted herself onto a high bed and rearranged her clothing for the nurse to perform the ultrasound scan, with me sitting on one side of my daughter and the nurse on the other. I watched, fascinated, as a jelly-like substance was smeared over Megan's abdomen and then the nurse moved the scanner, knowing precisely what she was looking for. She pointed to a monitor beside the bed.

'There's baby,' she said with a grin. Beautiful words, which the pretty young nurse must have the privilege of saying so many times. As she traced the spine of my grandchild with her finger, three pairs of eyes followed. Baby was curled up as expected and appeared to have its thumb in its mouth.

'Do you want to know the gender?' she asked.

'Yes, please!' We waited, holding our breath.

'Well, this is by no means a hundred per cent accurate, and the next scan will give a better indication, but it looks like a girl to me.' We all smiled; it wouldn't have mattered what the gender was. This baby was so very welcome and wanted.

Back in the car, Megan phoned James before we set off.

'It's a girl!' she shouted excitedly. 'Well, it's not a certainty, but it's what the nurse seems to think.' From the one-sided conversation I heard, it appeared James was delighted. I leaned towards her and whispered, 'Thank him for letting me go,' which she did before we left for home.

I spent the rest of the day with Megan and Sam, who we collected from nursery. He knew about the baby but didn't fully understand how long they would have to wait. Sam wanted a brother and asked if they could call him Triceratops, after his favourite dinosaur. The next few months would give his parents a chance to prepare Sam for being a big brother to a baby sister and hopefully persuade him to reconsider his choice of name.

2nd November

I had an early night last night, tired after the previous day during which I had laughed with my family and 'met' my first granddaughter. This morning, however, was the day for a visit to the local hospice. The irony of these two visits was not wholly lost on me, although I tried not to overthink it or compare the very real differences they represented. Yesterday was all about new life, marvelling at the wonders of a baby, while today I'm considering the end stages of my life and how I want to spend those final days.

Rachel had made the appointment to visit the hospice for me. During her visits she talked so positively about the place but I still wasn't sure what to expect. The word 'hospice' conjures up thoughts of death, dying, illness and sadness. But that isn't how Rachel perceives it, so I set off with a particular curiosity. The appointment was at eleven am and I'd chosen to go alone. Megan was working today but offered to take time off to accompany me, an offer I declined not yet wanting her to see images of what my future could be.

Driving into the grounds of Saint Bartholomew's Hospice, I was struck by the tranquil setting. The car crunched slowly over a gravel driveway as I followed the signs for visitor parking, gawping at the lovely gardens on each side. The recent rain was still on the ground, picking out the colours of the stones and reflecting the various shades of gold and amber. Although not a gardening enthusiast I can still appreciate a lovely garden and this was undoubtedly one of them. Not a huge site, perhaps about an acre in total, but the shrubs and trees looked magnificent, the beds were well-stocked with colourful winter pansies and the last of the chrysanthemums and dahlias. I could imagine how it must look in spring and summer, but I'll never know.

The building was in excellent repair for its age, which I guessed was late Victorian. The stonework appeared to have recently been cleaned, sandblasted probably, and the enormous wooden doors were a glossy black with shining brass fitments. Not knowing whether to ring the bell or wait, I rang, then tried the door, which opened readily. Inside, a warm lobby and bright, welcoming area held a long wooden desk from behind which a couple of middle-aged ladies lifted their heads to greet me. I smiled tentatively.

'Hello, welcome!' one of the ladies chirped. 'Are you Mrs Reid?'

'Yes,' I owned up, 'I think I'm to see Mrs Chapman?'

'That's right. I'll give her a buzz. Take a seat if you like.'

Mrs Chapman (call me Sylvia) came straight out of her office, a woman of about fortyish, tall, slim and with short-cropped blonde hair. Her smile was warm and genuine, and I took to her immediately. She introduced me to the two ladies at reception, names I promptly forgot, who were both volunteers and then we began the tour.

I don't quite know what I was expecting a hospice to look like, probably some kind of hospital with the addition of a few homely touches, flowers and cups of tea, perhaps? It was cosy and much more. The rooms were smaller than I expected and bore no resemblance to hospital wards. Sylvia talked with ease and maybe a little pride about what was on offer at St. Bartholomew's. It was a surprise to learn that only six beds were set aside for in-patients in single rooms, and not all of these were for end-stage patients. Respite care was accommodated here, too, perhaps to give carers a break or the patients themselves if they lived alone without support, and others came for a few days of pain management care during difficult times. The overall impression was of flexibility and every effort to be as accommodating as possible.

Complimentary therapies were practised here, too, massage and acupuncture to ease pain and relax muscles. We peered into one room fitted with a Jacuzzi, not in use at the time but immensely popular, according to Sylvia. Then there were diversional therapies, art and crafts, varied and tailored to patients' interests wherever possible. Some rooms had music, soothing melodies and big band sounds; all in all, it felt like a large home with many rooms.

A hairdresser worked in a small salon where she offered

hairdressing and manicures – she was busy as we passed, with two clients happily chatting away as they would in any other hairdressing salon. There were self-service facilities for tea and coffee, which we used before sitting in a couple of comfortable armchairs overlooking the gardens. I complimented Sylvia on the ethos and atmosphere of St. Bartholomew's and she appeared delighted at my approval.

A young boy, probably in his early teens, was sitting at the other side of the room with someone who could have been his mother, or perhaps a volunteer. They were playing Scrabble, the boy's bald head angled down towards the board as he studied the letters. A sudden shriek followed by raucous laughter informed us that he'd won the game. As he looked in our direction for an approving nod from Sylvia, his laughter seemed inconsistent with his appearance. The boy's skin was pale, almost translucent, with hair and eyebrows no more but this brave young boy could still laugh and enjoy the mundane pleasures of life.

'James comes for a few days each month for respite care while his parents have a break and give time to their other children,' Sylvia explained.

Suddenly my situation seemed so much less tragic than this child's. I've lived for nearly sixty wonderful years and had the joy of seeing my children develop into happy, healthy adults, whereas this boy was stricken down before he'd even started to live. I didn't ask about his prognosis; it was none of my business and I doubt Sylvia would have discussed it anyway, but I felt such empathy for his parents. To lose a child is not the natural order of life and must surely be one of the hardest things to bear.

While drinking the hot coffee, I asked a few more questions about the facility. Having seen the place and the positivity it emanated I was almost convinced that this was where I wanted to die. I know many people wish to die at home in their own bed, which I'd seriously considered, but now the hospice seemed a much better option for me, Megan, and Luke. I didn't want to play the role of the dying matriarch surrounded by family; it was depressing and unfair to them. Besides, I'm a bit of a coward and in the hospice, pain management was on hand with qualified experienced staff to help me and my family.

Sylvia explained just how flexible they could be. Naturally, patients couldn't always book in advance so the hospice worked on a daily basis offering care as the need arose. However, Sylvia did persuade me to take advantage of some of their complimentary therapies, and I fixed an appointment for a massage in just over a week. A little unsure of having this kind of treatment, I looked upon it as a good way to see more of the hospice's work and meet some of the people who might one day be caring for me.

After thanking Sylvia, I left with much to ponder, wondering how long it would be before I felt the need for end-of-life care. For the time being, I was managing well enough with family support and Rachel's visits, and as I didn't possess a crystal ball to predict my future, life would just have to be lived one day at a time.

TWENTY-TWO
HELEN

3rd November

From my window this morning, there was a strong sense of approaching winter and a light covering of early frost. The garden had shrugged off the last vestiges of autumn, and leaves carpeted the lawn, crisp and colourful in their golden hues. James had taken on the gardening chores, as finding a gardener proved difficult; they were more interested in larger projects and not the regular maintenance of a small family garden, particularly at this time of year. My son-in-law would be coming again at the weekend to give a final tidy-up before winter took hold.

Breakfast this morning was disturbed by a call from the matron at The Valley. Mum had had a restless night, followed by what the matron described as an outburst she wanted to discuss with me. I was due to visit again and told her I'd call after lunch.

As I seem to be doing quite often of late, I pottered around in my nightclothes, finishing breakfast and reading the paper before getting dressed. Gus has uncomplainingly accepted this change in routine and makes do with the garden, knowing we'll take our walk when I'm dressed.

By the time I set off to see Mum, the early frost had disappeared but the chill in the air reminded me how quickly time was passing – winter was most certainly making its presence felt. This year I dreaded the season more than ever; driving was becoming increasingly less appealing and if the weather turned too bad I could foresee many days when I'd not leave the house.

At the care home, I stopped by the office before going to Mum's room or seeking her out in the lounge. The matron greeted me with a smile and offered coffee and we sat balancing our cups and saucers, with me wondering what she wanted to say. I've always had a high regard for this lady who runs a good home, and from what I'd seen over the few years my mother had been there she treated both staff and patients well, with dignity and respect.

'I don't want you to worry about this, Helen, but your mother seems to have had some kind of episode during which she became somewhat violent, even more so than the last little outburst.' This kind lady related what sounded like a tantrum with my mother having 'trashed' (for want of a better word) her room. The matron was telling me gently, considering my feelings with genuine concern. As I began to apologise, she waved her hand.

'No, no, this is something which happens occasionally. There's no need to apologise.' We walked along to Mum's room, and I could see what had occurred, although it was mostly tidied up by then. The family photographs lay on the dressing table, in frames without glass, and other breakable items were missing. The matron explained how my mother started throwing things around and how most of the breakables were now destroyed.

She was almost embarrassed now, but I didn't blame her. The incident had apparently passed swiftly and Mum was taken to the lounge while the debris was cleared up.

Gathering up the photos, I followed the matron back to her office where I anticipated her explaining how they could no longer care for Mum. I was wrong. The matron had a plan to alter Mum's medication more permanently. In effect, she would be prescribed tranquillisers designed to subdue these violent outbursts. My agreement to seek the doctor's advice on this was required, a decision I readily made, knowing the alternative would be to move my mother to a secure mental health facility, a move she'd most likely take badly. With a sigh of relief, I went to the lounge, scanning the chairs to see Mum happily humming to herself, seated by the window and twisting the fabric of her skirt around her fingers. I kissed her brow and she looked up, startled to see me.

'Is dinner ready?' was all she asked as I knelt before her. There was no point in asking about the morning's incident. It was already forgotten. Instead, I took her hand, unwinding the fabric from her fingers as she looked through me, seeing another person, not her daughter whose heart was almost breaking because I couldn't make things right for her or myself.

The drive home allowed me time to think. My mother no longer knew who I or any other family member was. She existed in the home, well cared for but without any sense of where or who she was. And here I was, only too aware of what was happening in my body but as helpless as Mum to do anything about it. I wondered which one of us had the better deal.

4th November

After describing the visit to her grandmother, Megan

attempted to persuade me not to let it upset me and offered to take on future visits, which in truth seemed only a duty at times. But I wasn't quite ready to say goodbye to Mum. I had a crushing feeling of handing all my cares over to my daughter, and the sense of guilt was almost overwhelming. We hadn't discussed what would happen to Gus after D-Day, but there was no doubt Megan would take him; she loved him as much as I did. It felt all wrong somehow, but there was nothing I could do – my daughter would be left with the remnants of my life to dispose of as she felt best.

Rachel visited again today, breezing in, bringing her zest for life which I found strangely encouraging and I wondered if all her patients appreciated her wisdom and skill. We discussed the hospice visit and Rachel was delighted I'd found it helpful. I told her of my decision to go there for the last few days and she assured me that my family and I would be very welcome when the time came. I also found myself telling her about my mother and the day's events. Rachel asked what my relationship had been like before Mum's illness took her away and I happily described the caring, gentle lady she'd been and the bond of love we'd shared. Having previously talked much about my early life with Andrew and the twins, talking now about my childhood felt strangely cathartic, making me see how blessed I have been. Again, Rachel listened patiently, nodding in encouragement and occasionally asking questions which prompted other thoughts and memories.

'There's something special about a mother-daughter relationship,' she said, reminding me that she too was close to her mother, who must be very proud of the caring sensitive woman Rachel had become. I fully agreed and asked if her mother was still looking after her children.

'Yes, the girls love her. Sometimes I don't get a look-in;

they're so close.' But her smile showed pleasure at the arrangement they had.

'It was good to meet Megan at the hospital – she's very like you, isn't she?'

'So I'm told, yet I can't always see it myself.'

'Take it from me; she favours you in many ways.' It made me happy to think so.

After discussing the medication and Rachel making a few tweaks to the dosage, she left to move on to her next patient and I took Gus out for his last walk of the day before settling down with a cup of tea to watch the television.

5th November

Tonight there will be fireworks, and Gus will hate it. He's a dog and doesn't understand such matters, so I shall do what I've done each bonfire night since Gus came – turn the television to its loudest setting and wait for the celebrations and inevitable noise to pass.

I intended to spend another quiet day at home to continue with Christmas preparations. Having already baked several batches of my family's favourite cakes, which were in the freezer, today I decided to make a Christmas cake, but the doorbell heralded a change of plan. My heart sank when I opened the door to find DS Greenwood and DC Hamilton. I'd been working hard on erasing all thoughts about the police and what might happen and my initial thought was that their presence on my doorstep could only herald bad news. Yet as they entered my lounge, DC Hamilton had a trace of a smile on her face, undoubtedly a good sign. As before, DS Greenwood opened the dialogue.

'Mrs Reid, we've spent considerable time investigating your

claims.' It sounded like a reprimand, designed to make me feel guilty perhaps.

'All without success, so the CPS has decided not to proceed with the case due to lack of evidence and, er, your own situation.' His expression was of disappointment at giving me this relatively good news but Rose Hamilton was smiling more openly now and added her opinion.

'This isn't to say that we apportion blame in any way to you. However, the lapse of time and the lack of a direct witness make it difficult to proceed. Mr Wheeler is known to us, and we would have welcomed the opportunity to pursue this with him, but without anything more concrete it would be a waste of time and resources.'

'So, are you telling me you believe my account of things rather than Rob's?' I asked.

'Yes,' Rose said. 'If we could have taken this any further we'd have done so – it may have helped in other inquiries in which Mr Wheeler's name crops up, but it's not to be so for the time being there's nothing else we can do.'

It was a huge relief to know they actually believed my account and not Rob's lies but a disappointment that Rob seemed to have avoided the consequences of his actions once again. This decision may let me off the hook, but I've still not achieved what I set out to do – to make recompense for my part in the fatal accident.

'I don't suppose Susan Wheeler has been to see you?' I asked.

'No.' DS Greenwood frowned. 'Have you been in touch with her?'

'Yes, I went to see her to try and persuade her to tell you the truth.'

'Mrs Reid, you shouldn't have had any contact with the Wheelers while we investigated the matter.' His face darkened.

'I'm sorry, I never thought of it that way.' Stupid me, I should have known it wouldn't help.

'What did Mrs Wheeler say to you, Helen?' Rose spoke kindlier.

'Initially, she wasn't very forthcoming and clearly frightened of Rob. She admitted that he hits her and was keen to warn me not to go there again for my own safety. Susan seems to think he's aligned himself with some criminals or criminal activity in Leeds.'

DS Greenwood suddenly looked interested. 'Did she mention anything specific, a name perhaps?'

'No, but she says he gets plenty of money and she doesn't dare to ask where it comes from.' My answer sounded lame even to me, but the DS looked interested.

'Do you think she'd talk to us?' Rose asked.

'I'm not sure. Susan's frightened of Rob, a fear which seems well-founded, and I don't think she'd want to risk losing her comfortable lifestyle.'

'Have you any way of contacting her without Wheeler knowing?' The sergeant was suddenly almost animated, as if a dozen or more thoughts were whirling in his brain.

'No. I left a number with her – an old mobile number. Susan can contact me but the only way I could see her is to go back to the house.'

'Not advisable!' Rose seemed concerned, her words emphathic.

'If you hear from her again, will you let us know? If we could charge him with another offence, we could probably revisit the hit-and-run charge.'

After I assured him I would, DS Greenwood stood to leave

An enormous feeling of relief that the police would not be pressing any charges against me lightened my spirit. They gave a distinct impression they'd not believed Rob's lies, my only grumble being that it would have been nice to have known sooner rather than being left to imagine the worst.

After this unexpected encounter, I went straight to the kitchen to distract my thoughts by immersing myself in making my very last Christmas cake.

TWENTY-THREE
HELEN

6th November

Today was the day for my second visit to Saint Bartholomew's Hospice. Strange though it may seem I'd never had a massage before unless you count Andrew massaging my shoulders after a tiring day at work.

Hesitantly, I entered the hospice's beautiful building where Sylvia stood near the reception desk and turned to greet me warmly. Ushering me towards one of the many small rooms to introduce me to Claire, who was to be my masseuse, Sylvia assured me I would enjoy the experience. Claire was perhaps in her early twenties with an obvious penchant for bright colours. Her hair was purple, twisted into a knot on top of her head with rainbow wisps sticking out at all angles. Her choice of clothes for work was a bright-green jumper with multicoloured-striped sleeves, a short red skirt, and black tights. I found it impossible not to smile at this girl whose face was made up almost as colourfully as her clothes with a generous amount of blusher and eyeshadow in purple and yellow. Strangely it blended well and as this kindly girl took my coat and launched into an endless stream of chatter, I found her quite charming. Taking my clothes off in front of a stranger felt a little awkward, but she gave me a clean white sheet to cover my modesty and everything was done very sensitively.

Claire's voice generated an almost hypnotic effect on me as she worked on my body and I soon relaxed beneath her touch. As I lay on my back, Claire started at my head, fingers gently massaging my scalp, then my temples, and down to the rest of my face. I'd opted for lavender and rose-scented oils, which she rubbed gently into my body. I relaxed and yielded to her expert touch, helped by the whisper of soothing music playing somewhere in the background. Claire's constant chatter was comforting and undemanding as she asked no questions. It was a little late to convert to the benefits of massage and I wished I'd discovered it sooner.

After forty-five minutes of unhurried, gentle and professional massage, I could see why Claire fitted in at the hospice. She was a delightful, colourful asset to their work and I hoped to have another session with her before too long.

When Sylvia appeared again, she persuaded me to have a manicure, telling me that one of their volunteers had just arrived to offer her services for a patient who'd cancelled at the last minute. After thanking Claire, I moved into another room to be pampered some more with a manicure.

My nails were kept relatively short these days and I only occasionally treated myself to a manicure, so this was an extra. Marie too, was young and almost as chatty as Claire. Again, no questions were asked and I felt under no obligation to say anything unless I wished to do so.

On leaving Saint Bartholomew's I felt more relaxed than I'd done for days. The massage served to ease those tense muscles and even relieved some of the pain in my lower back. The manicure was an unexpected extra luxury, and as I rarely bothered with such pampering these days, it lifted my mood.

Driving across the gravel I briefly wondered how long it would be before I became a resident in this lovely old house.

7th November

From the kitchen, I heard a faint ringing. It took me a few seconds to work out that the unfamiliar ringtone was Andrew's old mobile phone, which lay where I'd put it on the shelf below the coffee table in the lounge. Hurrying to pick it up, I knew there was only one person it could be, Susan Wheeler. Holding the phone to my ear, muffled sobs indicated all was not well.

'Susan? What is it? I'm listening.' I was floundering and hadn't a clue what to say. I needed Susan to talk to me, but she seemed incapable of doing anything but cry.

'Are you okay?' Stupid question! She wouldn't be in such a state if she were.

'Has Rob hurt you? You can always call the police.'

'No, not the police!' The mention of the police seemed to scare my one-time friend, perhaps even more than Rob himself.

'Tell me what happened.' I spoke calmly, though feeling quite the opposite.

'The police came yesterday, asking me about Rob's income and his friends in Leeds. How could they know about his involvement with people in Leeds?'

I was glad she couldn't see my face, flushed with shame as if I'd betrayed her confidence. Susan continued, 'Ricky arrived as they were leaving and wanted to know why they were there. I told him they were still asking questions about the accident. He told Rob they'd been and he was furious when he got home early this morning. She paused, her breathing still erratic. I could only imagine how terrified she must be feeling.

'He... said if I'd told them anything he'd kill me! I think he means it, Helen.' The sobbing started again.

'Susan, you don't have to stay with that monster. Why don't you pack a bag and get out while you can?'

'It's easy for you to say, but where would I go?'

'Go to the police, tell them what happened and they'll help. There are places they can take you where you'll be safe. You don't have to be Rob's punchbag anymore.'

'I honestly thought he was going to kill me this time. If I go to the police, will you come with me?'

The request threw me. Didn't I have enough worries without having to go back to Grimethorpe – the very thought made me feel nauseous but after a short silence, I heard myself answer yes. It was about ten in the morning and after checking that Rob would almost certainly be out for the rest of the day, I told Susan I'd be with her as soon as possible. Before leaving, I considered ringing DS Greenwood but decided not to; he would only attempt to dissuade me from going and might even use the opportunity to visit Susan again while she was vulnerable. I couldn't do that to her.

The traffic was light for which I was grateful. Nevertheless, it was a struggle to focus on the road as my mind was unsuccessfully seeking ideas or words which might be appropriate in this dire situation. There were no cars outside the Wheelers' house as I drove into the cul-de-sac, so I went to the head of the road and turned my car around to face the way out – in case I needed to leave in haste. With shaking legs and a dry mouth, I forced myself to approach the front door and ring the bell.

Susan must have been watching as she answered immediately. The sight of her face was a shock; her bottom lip was swollen with a cut, still bleeding, at the side of her mouth. Her puffy eyes could have been from crying but the left one also looked red and swollen – Rob was most probably responsible for that too. As I followed her through the house and into the kitchen, I drew water to fill the kettle while Susan sat down, head in hands and elbows supported on the table, dabbing at her mouth with a stained and crumpled tissue. I moved to the cupboard where previously I'd seen her reach for cups and soon we both had tea in front of us, Susan's with a generous amount of sugar stirred into it. Only then could I take in her other injuries – a badly swollen wrist and alarming bruising to her neck – small, dark circles made from the pressure of her husband's fingers, a gruesome necklace of tiny bruises.

'You need to go to hospital, your wrist could be broken.' My words brought a look of panic to her face. We both knew hospitals ask awkward questions.

'Has he done this before, I mean, as bad as this?'

She shook her head. 'No. I usually get out of the way when he starts, but he followed me upstairs this morning.' Susan's left eye was showing signs of bruising – I hardly dared to imagine what she'd look like in a few more hours. The cut at the side of her mouth was still bleeding and probably needed a stitch to enable it to heal.

'Shall I call the police?' I felt pretty much out of my depth in this situation. Ironically the only other time in my life when I'd been as scared as this was also connected to Rob Wheeler.

'No! He'll kill me if I go to the police.'

'He might kill you if you don't!' I had to persuade her to take action for her safety. 'What will happen when he comes home later today?'

'I don't know!' The tears flowed again. I moved to the other side of the table and embraced Susan's trembling body, feeling utterly helpless.

We both heard the car, and I stiffened, hoping it wasn't Rob. But it was!

The door banged open, and he shouted his wife's name with an angry voice and the tell-tale slur of the inebriated. We both froze where we were, hardly daring to breathe. Rob was in the hall and was bound to see us when he moved forward.

'Well, well, what have we here?' The sneer on his face and his dark, scowling eyes told us Rob's anger had not diminished in the slightest. Although terrified, I felt strangely protective towards Susan who was shaking quite violently. I remained beside her as Rob approached the table and tried to grab his wife's arm to drag her up. She screamed with pain and I used the weight of my body to push him away while at the same time trying to shield Susan from his outburst. Rob stumbled slightly, regaining his footing and turning his attention towards me.

My instinct was to run, to make a dash for the front door and get to the car as quickly as possible. I reached into my pocket and felt the reassuring cool metal of the car keys but I knew I couldn't leave Susan to face her husband's wrath alone. As he stepped forward again, Rob grinned, his crooked, nicotine-stained teeth bared like an animal ready to pounce. As his large rough hands reached around my neck, I staggered backwards and Susan used the opportunity to run from the room. I hoped she'd call the police as I heard her running upstairs.

Still holding the keys in my hand, I pulled them out and reaching for Rob's face, dug them into his cheek as hard as I could, dragging them down the flabby flesh on his face. He yelped like a wounded dog as blood trickled from the deep wound I'd made. At least my actions made him release his hands from around my neck, but in an instant he came back at me, obscenities spitting from his mouth and steely determination in those dark eyes. There was hardly time to think about what to do and the keys were useless as a weapon to stop him altogether.

Looking around the kitchen, I saw a knife block on the work

surface. Almost falling towards it, I managed to pull the largest knife from its resting place and gripping the wooden handle, waved it in front of Rob's face. He stopped, scowled at me momentarily and then started laughing.

'You wouldn't dare!' he mocked, and was probably right. It'd been instinctive to scratch his face with the keys, but to plunge a knife into another human being's body was something I doubted I could do, even to protect myself.

The moment seemed to last an hour as we stared at each other. I could see hatred and arrogance in Rob's eyes, and I'm sure he would see only fear and uncertainty in mine. Finally, he moved, lurching quickly towards me, grabbing and twisting my wrist in the same firm movement. Pain shot through my arm and I dropped the knife. Before I could duck down to retrieve it, Rob reached it first. I stumbled backwards, but there was nowhere to go – I was cornered, hurting, and scared out of my wits!

Rob appeared to relax now, knowing he had the upper hand and his quarry was helpless. Moving forward and still holding the knife, he pressed his body into mine. I felt sick from his proximity. Then, raising his hand to my face, he pressed the flat side of the steel blade into my cheek. His other hand was toying with my hair. I was frozen with fear, utterly powerless.

'Shall we have some fun now?' he said, grinning with saliva dribbling down his chin. 'For old times' sake?'

'Let her go!' I'd almost forgotten Susan was still in the house and so apparently had her husband. He laughed as he turned towards her and asked, 'And are you going to make me?'

The reply stunned us both.

'Yes!' Susan shouted and lifted both hands to shoulder height to reveal a handgun, the sight of which made Rob release his grip on me.

'No!' he shouted, staggering towards his wife.

I had no idea a gun would sound so loud; perhaps it

wouldn't be, outside, but we were in a confined space. Rob fell to the floor. Susan had dropped her arms forty-five degrees before pulling the trigger and consequently, the bullet ripped into her husband's right knee. As he writhed on the floor screaming in agony, Susan flopped onto a chair, holding her wrist which must have been excruciating after firing the gun.

Of the three of us I seemed to be the only one relatively unscathed, so it was up to me to take action. Susan had dropped the gun on the floor and I kicked it away, fearing Rob might recover sufficiently to reach for it, then I hurried into the hall and picked up the telephone to dial 999.

A strange feeling of being outside the whole situation had taken over, and I acted robotically, as if unconnected to this absurd scenario. I'd recovered sufficiently to ask for police and an ambulance, then to hide the gun behind a hall chair, and finally to attempt to stem the blood flow from Rob's knee. Grabbing a hand towel and tea cloth, I wrapped them around his leg, causing considerable pain which I took a guilty pleasure in ignoring.

It was a relief when the sound of car sirens screeched the arrival of two police officers to the usually quiet neighbourhood. I was happy to step back and let them take control, comforting Susan as best as I could and only then aware of my rapidly beating heart and trembling limbs.

An ambulance was quickly in attendance with flashing lights alerting the whole neighbourhood that something was seriously wrong. After an initial examination, the paramedics loaded a whining Rob onto a stretcher, with one of the police officers accompanying him. The remaining officer, realising Susan also needed medical attention, rang for a second ambulance and backup. Once medical needs were taken care of the police officer swiftly assessed the situation and as I appeared to be the only person coherent enough to answer questions, he began to quiz me for details of the morning's events.

Firstly, I took him into the hall and pointed out the gun which I didn't wish to handle or even see again. Taking a plastic evidence bag from his pocket and without touching it, he put it inside the bag and sealed it. We returned to the lounge, where I sat beside Susan, who was now rocking back and forth like a frightened child, tearful and moaning. As I put my arm around her, she leaned on my shoulder and closed her eyes as I related the awful events of the last hour for the benefit of the attending police officer.

We were soon disturbed by the second ambulance arriving at the same time as DS Greenwood and DC Hamilton. As the ambulance was about to take Susan away, I asked if I might go with her. DS Greenwood refused, looking far from happy and saying I must stay to answer questions. Rose Hamilton was delegated to accompany Susan while I remained in the house, stunned by everything which had transpired.

To give him due credit, DS Greenwood treated me with a degree of sensitivity. We were back in the lounge, the kitchen was a mess but the sergeant didn't want anything moved for the present. I asked if I could get my medication from my bag and he thoughtfully brought me a glass of water. I took some painkillers and then told him everything I could, doing my best to answer his questions. The detective made occasional notes but I knew I'd have to go over it again in a more formal statement.

Being incredibly weary I just wanted to go home, sink into my bed and pretend this had all been a terrible nightmare. DS Greenwood asked if I could drive and as I considered it, the answer was no. My hands and legs still trembled – it was doubtful I'd be safe to drive. He fished out his mobile and tapped in a number, asking for a car and two officers who arrived within half an hour. Names were given, but I could take nothing in and allowed a young PC to drive me home in my car while the second officer followed to take his colleague back to the station.

It was 4.30pm when we arrived at my home. The officer insisted on seeing me inside and only left after assurances that I'd be fine and just needed to rest. Once alone, I let Gus into the garden while making tea and toast – all I seemed to exist on now. Within an hour of arriving home, I was sound asleep with Gus curled up beside me on the bed.

TWENTY-FOUR
SUSAN

I awoke in a hospital bed, sore, stiff and afraid. It wasn't the same kind of fear as yesterday when I thought Rob would kill me, but still a very tangible fear of the future – an uncertainty of what would happen to me next. It's painfully clear that my life will never be the same again, all bridges are burned, and I'll somehow have to find a way to build a new life.

The young detective constable stayed at the hospital with me for almost two hours yesterday, putting my mind at rest about Rob's whereabouts. I imagined him coming to find me during the night to finish off what he'd started, but she assured me Rob had been transferred to another hospital to undergo surgery on his leg, and when he was fit enough to leave, he would be taken into police custody for questioning. So, after my wrist was set in a plaster cast (it was broken as Helen thought) I tried to go over what had transpired and how I came to shoot my husband.

Strangely, I hadn't thought about the trouble I could be in for shooting Rob until after the event but when I mentioned the gun to the DC, she told me not to worry and concentrate on getting better. This morning, however, I looked worse. The bruises on my face had darkened, with both cheekbones almost black and the left eye so swollen I couldn't open it. Yellowish bruises with distinctive finger marks adorned my neck like an ugly amber necklace. At least I'd slept, helped by medication which I took readily, longing for the oblivion of sleep. Thankfully I was in a side room away from the central ward so didn't have to fend off any awkward questions about my injuries, and if the nurses knew the circumstances of my admission they were very discreet about it.

A pretty young nurse helped me to my feet – she was bright and chatty and, when asked, said I could probably leave the hospital later in the day if the doctor was happy with my cast after his rounds. I almost begged to stay, suddenly wanting to be looked after and fussed over, but my injuries consisted mainly of bruising, and a broken wrist didn't warrant occupying a hospital bed. Breakfast tasted good, unsurprising as I'd eaten nothing the day before. Afterwards, I lay back on the bed and willed the doctor to go on his rounds or forget about me altogether as I languished in bed, tucked away in this safe little room.

DC Hamilton appeared in the doorway, smiling as she knocked on the open door. 'Hi, how are you feeling this morning, Susan?'

Surprising even myself I burst into tears, prompting her to rush to the bedside and pat my arm. 'Hey, don't cry; you're safe now.' I think the poor girl was embarrassed but I couldn't help myself – the detective and nurses were kind – Helen had been kind and I wasn't used to it. Stupid fool that I am, I didn't know how to react to kindness. After pulling myself together, I asked questions, wanting to know where I stood regarding the shooting and if Rob would soon be out and about. The DC did her best to answer.

'I've spoken to DS Greenwood who thinks it's a clear case of self-defence and as you were also protecting Mrs Reid, who was being attacked, I don't think you have anything to worry about – unless the gun is yours? We've checked for a permit and there isn't a firearm registered to you or your husband.'

'No way, it's not mine! I found it a few weeks ago in a drawer. I didn't even know Rob had it until then and didn't dare ask him about it.' I think she believed me – this time I was keen to tell the truth. 'Will he go to prison when he gets out of the hospital, on remand or something, or will he be let go?' My mind didn't want to consider the possibility of Rob being released; he'd surely come after me.

'It all depends on what charges we can bring. We've known about some of your husband's activities for a while now, but we need proof to charge him. Is there anything you can help us with, Susan?'

Even if I wanted to help, in all honesty, I could think of nothing. My husband was always careful to keep his dealings well-hidden, even from me, and I told her so.

'If you're prepared to testify against him, we could charge him with assault, possibly even attempted murder?' She looked at me hopefully but it wasn't an easy decision. If I knew for sure Rob would be locked away for a long time I would do it, but if he was going to be out on licence or whatever, I wouldn't be safe even with a restraining order. Fudging the issue, I told her I'd think about it and moved on to ask what would happen to me. I couldn't go home; Rob might not be there but Ricky was a few blocks away – Ricky, who always did his brother's bidding, it wouldn't be safe to return home and I told the DC.

'There's a place we can take you, a refuge where you'll be helped to start a new life. It's in Barnsley, and they have facilities to help with various things – counselling, financial advice and even clothes if needed.'

I wasn't completely sold on the idea but having someone around to help me get sorted out would be good, and what other options did I have? The more I thought about it, the more it appealed – just to get me on my feet. DC Hamilton was looking at me, waiting for me to speak.

'Talking of clothes, they're probably going to discharge me today and I could do with going home to get some things.' I had plenty of clothes at home and also some money hidden away. 'Could you come with me? I don't want to go alone.'

'Yes, it's no problem. Look, give me a ring when you know what time you'll be discharged and I'll take you home for your things then run you over to Barnsley. Is that okay?'

It was more than okay; it made me feel safe and when DC Hamilton left I began seriously considering my future.

The doctor appeared after lunch and gave me a thorough examination, mainly looking for signs of concussion, although I assured him I hadn't hit my head when I fell. Eventually, he decided to discharge me. I rang DC Hamilton and after a quick shower, I dressed in yesterday's clothes and waited for her to arrive.

It only occurred to me on the way back to Grimethorpe that I didn't have my house keys.

'Actually, I've got a set in my bag,' DC Hamilton explained. 'DS Greenwood locked up after we left, with keys he found on the hall table.' So the problem was sorted.

Pulling up outside my home brought an unexpected jumble of emotions. I'd loved this house when we first moved in, with its luxurious modern fittings and well-proportioned rooms but now it almost repelled me, no longer feeling like home. In my naivety I'd thought the house would herald a new era for Rob and me – we'd become closer and happier. Now I viewed it from a different perspective – the prison where I'd been kept with no purpose and very little joy in my life. I could no longer understand why the house or the mundane, meaningless existence had ever appealed to me. My life in that house had been one of isolation; the neighbours didn't bother with me and I had no friends to speak of. For years I'd been lying to myself, perceiving the house, the furnishings and the clothes as symbols of a good life. Pretending Rob loved me was also a fantasy I chose to believe because I desperately wanted it to be true. I should have left him the first time he hit me, but I lacked the courage and clung to my home and possessions for comfort, fearing the unknown. Better the devil you know, I'd thought.

Entering the front door, I was now strangely hesitant. Knowing Rob was still in the hospital, Ricky was my primary fear – he might turn up at any time. He kept a set of keys and often brought and picked up packages for his brother. I only hoped Ricky would be aware of recent events and would keep well away, which he would if he had any sense, especially if he knew of the police involvement.

As we passed the open kitchen door, the mess from the previous day stunned me. Much of the incident was still hazy in my mind and I caught my breath at the thought of how things could have turned out. Broken crockery, upended chairs and blood covered the floor. It was like someone else's house or a television drama with me as an onlooker. I had no desire to clean it up and restore order, neither knowing nor caring what would happen to this house in the future, and it was a strangely empowering feeling.

DC Hamilton waited downstairs while I went to pack a few clothes. Opening my wardrobe, I viewed the contents (most of which had never been worn) hanging on several rails. They were garments bought in Leeds or Barnsley on one of my trips there, paid for with the cash Rob gave me when he was in a good mood or after hitting me – I always thought it was his way of saying sorry. We always used cash, and it never struck me as unusual that neither of us possessed a bank account or credit card. Most of the garments before me were impractical, totally useless. I'd bought several evening dresses on a whim and would never have occasion to wear them. At the time I was trying to convince myself that one day I would wear them, one day my life would be like the one I dreamed about in which Rob and I enjoyed a busy social life with dozens of friends. Hell, the lies we tell ourselves. The shoes were frivolous, pretty and expensive but again mostly unworn – I probably couldn't even walk in them if I tried.

Shopping was my comfort, and choosing clothes was the only decision I could make without consulting my husband. Pushing these unfulfilled dreams from my mind, I pulled out some more practical items, trousers, jumpers and jackets which had been bought for comfort and wouldn't be out of place at the refuge I was going to.

In the bathroom I quickly gathered a few essentials, dropping them all into a brand-new vanity case which I'd never had occasion to use before.

Back in the bedroom, pulling a chair over to the wardrobe, I balanced precariously on it to reach the highest shelf and lift down an old shoebox. Carefully lifting the lid, I removed the rolls of money which over the years I'd squirrelled away for a rainy day. It was undoubtedly pouring down now. I stuffed the rolls of money down the sides of my case, hiding them from sight and making a mental note of how much there must be. They were all twenty-pound notes, each a roll of fifty notes secured with an elastic band. In total, fifteen rolls which amounted to fifteen thousand pounds. The amount staggered me – if asked, I'd be unable to say why I'd stashed so much money. Perhaps deep down I'd always known my marriage was insecure and a self-preservation instinct had kicked in. Or maybe my overcautious mother's influence remained deep within – she always kept cash in an old tea caddy at the back of the cupboard. Whatever the reason, I was grateful now to have it. It was also beginning to dawn on me that if I'd been able to gather such a large amount from the money Rob gave me, how much more had he kept for himself? Quite honestly, I didn't want to think about my husband anymore. We'd lived together more out of habit than love; he needed people around him with someone waiting at home and I'd been content to be that person – but not anymore.

Going downstairs with my bags, I found DC Hamilton in the study looking out of the window.

'I'm presuming this is Rob's room?' she asked and I nodded.

'Will you give us permission to search the house, Susan? It might help us to learn more about Rob's activities and save the time and trouble of getting a search warrant?'

It no longer mattered to me, so I nodded my consent.

'Keep the keys you have, if you like. I can get them back later.' I was unsure if I'd ever need or want to come back here; recent events had completely transformed my thinking. It was glaringly evident things would never return to how they were before. We left the house and made our way out of Grimethorpe, heading toward Barnsley.

TWENTY-FIVE
HELEN

8th November

Is it any wonder I felt terrible when I awoke this morning? After being up a couple of times through the night to visit the bathroom, I'd immediately sunk back into a deep, heavy sleep but it was time to get up and let Gus out, after which I showered, dressed and had something to eat. It was impossible to clear my mind of yesterday's events and my whole body seemed to be screaming out at me to rest; the pain was at its very worst.

Megan rang mid-morning to ask if we could meet in town for coffee and was naturally concerned when I declined, wanting to come to see me when I admitted to feeling unwell. I put her off, saying I'd lie down for a few hours and Rachel would be coming early in the afternoon. As ever, I hated keeping my daughter at arm's length but being so weak and in pain made me vulnerable, and I still wasn't ready to tell her about that shameful time in my past. Today, I questioned if I would ever do so. Megan offered to come round later in the afternoon with Sam, to which I agreed, asking if she could take

Gus out for his walk. I didn't want him to suffer because of my illness. With my day mapped out, I lay down and fell into a deep restful sleep.

Rachel arrived in the early afternoon, her cheerful presence welcome, so much that I felt somewhat overcome and embarrassed myself by crying. My wonderful nurse sat beside me and put an arm around my shoulder, saying nothing and simply being there for me. As the tears dried, the apologies tumbled out, stopped immediately by Rachel who said, 'I hoped we'd passed the stage of needing to apologise to each other. A good cry is sometimes appropriate; none of us can be strong all the time, Helen.'

She was right and apologising for apologising, we laughed and the moment passed. My lovely nurse instinctively knew I was feeling dreadful, emotionally and physically, and suggested it might be time to change to a stronger medication. I admitted to not liking the idea.

'Would it help to talk about it?' she asked, and I believed it would. So finally I decided to confide in someone – a person I knew would not judge my actions or betray my confidence.

It wasn't easy to know where to start, but the words fell out, a cathartic experience once I began. Rachel listened in silence as I explained my quest to redress a crime I'd played a part in long ago, and how this led me to visit the police and admit my culpability. Recalling the first visit to Rob and Susan prompted a shudder – then I moved on to the interview at Barnsley police station and the subsequent visit from the police after Rob had turned things around and accused me of being the driver. My ramblings probably made little sense – I was still shaken from the awful events of the previous day. Rachel nodded patiently, piecing things together, and I could almost feel her empathy as she grappled to understand the impact of these recent events.

'And are the police going to accept this man's word?' she asked. I related the more recent visit from them and how there was insufficient evidence to bring charges. And then there was yesterday to describe – Susan's call and apparent distress. A slight frown crossed Rachel's face when I admitted to going to see my one-time best friend.

Perhaps I generalised much of the story but needed to be more specific about the previous day's violence. When I reached the part about the gun, it seemed incredulous, even to me and I'd witnessed it first-hand. As I finished the account, Rachel took my hand in hers.

'Helen, you must take more care of yourself. I can see how this has snowballed but you're not well enough to be so involved. Please let the police sort it out from now on. You're not up to playing Miss Marple, are you?'

'I know, and hopefully I can put it all behind me, although it hasn't achieved what I initially set out to do – to make recompense to the poor man's family.'

'What poor man, Helen, you've lost me now.' Rachel frowned.

The phone rang before I could explain – the mobile phone, which could only be Susan. Rising to answer, I quickly said, 'The cyclist killed that night by Rob's car.'

Susan had so much to tell me and I wondered if I should offer to call her back, but then I didn't have a number and it sounded as if she was on a payphone. I looked at Rachel and shrugged, a kind of 'what can I do?' shrug. Rachel, with such a quizzical look on her face, stood and whispered, 'I'll leave you to your call, Helen.' She left, closing the door quietly and I regretted not finishing our conversation.

Susan continued to talk. My old friend was at a hostel for domestic abuse victims and wanted to tell me all about it. She must have felt better and sounded quite animated at times, having been given her own little bedsit in a complex which housed fifteen women at any one time. There was a shared kitchen and Susan appeared to enjoy the company. Some of the women had children, which again seemed to please her. I asked if she'd heard how Rob was, and her answer was that she neither knew or cared.

As Susan continued to talk, her voice seemed to be coming from a great distance and the images, still fresh in my mind from yesterday, felt unreal. It appeared my old friend either didn't consider yesterday's events as horrifying as I did or was deliberately avoiding thinking about them, in denial, perhaps?

Feeling increasingly detached from Susan, Rob and the police, I listened for a few more minutes before telling her someone was at the door and I needed to go. The someone was Megan, Sam tripping in behind his mother.

'Sorry, Mum, did I disturb your call?'

'No, love, it was just an old friend. How are you both?' Although an effort, it was also grounding to turn my attention to my daughter and grandson. They were real and present with me; yesterday was in the past and strangely surreal. Gus seemed to know he'd get his walk and wagged his tail in all directions, whining until Megan brought his lead.

'Can I stay with Grandma?' Sam asked. I nodded consent, Sam would soon cheer me up with his constant little boy chatter. Then, as Megan and Gus left, he asked for a story, which usually meant at least four and went to the bookshelf to choose his favourites. Sam climbed onto my knee, shuffling around to get comfortable and passed me the first book, *The Gruffalo*. His warm little body was comforting as I wrapped my arms around him and began the story, breathing in the smell of sunshine and wind in his hair and wishing the moment could last forever.

We read three books twice each before his mother returned, then Sam jumped down to play with Gus. My daughter put the kettle on to boil and I watched her moving around, trying to capture another mental snapshot to store in my mind and replay at will. When we were seated with our drinks and Sam was happily rummaging through a box of Lego, Megan brought up the subject of Gus.

'If you feel he's becoming too much for you, Mum, you know we'll have him. Sam loves him to bits, and James has always wanted a pet.'

I smiled my thanks, but I was not yet ready to let go of Gus, and today was the first time I'd not felt up to walking him. I agreed to let her know when the time was right. My daughter and son-in-law have both been so generous; this offer is one of several they've made in their attempt to make my life easier. They've even suggested I move into their home to allow them to take care of me, a tempting offer, but I think I'd like to stay put for as long as possible. I feel close to Andrew here. If I stop trying to live a normal life, it will be giving up – and I refuse to give up while I have the strength to continue.

I described my recent visit to the hospice and told Megan of my decision to spend my last days there. Tears ran down her face as she listened; this was as hard for her as it was for me, maybe harder? Perhaps I would stay with them for a while before going into the hospice, but I didn't want to be a burden – the hospice is undoubtedly the best place for me to spend those last days. Sam demanded our attention to admire his handiwork, a Lego tractor, and the subject was closed. I hated being the one to cause so much distress to my family but until D-Day there are days still to be lived, and I intend to do just that.

When Megan left, I rang Rachel's office number, hoping to catch her before she finished for the day. The lady who answered told me she'd already left but offered to leave a message for her to ring me the following day. I told her it wasn't important and not to bother with a message. I almost felt resentful towards Susan for depriving me of time with Rachel, but it wasn't her fault and I needed to let go of these intrusive, negative feelings. They seemed to be creeping in on occasion and I don't want to clutter my mind with such trivia.

TWENTY-SIX
SUSAN

The young constable, DC Rose Hamilton, was helpful beyond what could reasonably be expected of a police officer. When she brought me to the refuge three weeks ago, I was unsure if it was what I wanted, yet there was little choice as I couldn't return home when the hospital discharged me – it wasn't the safe place it had previously been.

My feelings towards my home and husband have been entirely turned upside down over the last few weeks – life had little purpose other than shopping, keeping the house in order and pacifying Rob when he was in a mood. Strangely, now I'm here, I can see it all too clearly, almost like an outsider looking at someone else's life. Yet there's nothing or no one to blame but myself. I've allowed life to turn around me while I sat on the sidelines observing, or perhaps it would be more accurate to say I sat on the sofa and ate. Eating and shopping were my comforts over the years, why has it taken until now to realise neither of them made me truly happy?

This place is full of women, each with a story to tell and most with bruises to illustrate it. If my clothes didn't fit on arrival, my colourful face certainly did. It feels so strange having others in such proximity. Yes, I have my tiny bedroom and shower room where I can be alone, but surprisingly I enjoy the company. If anyone suggested before that I was an abused wife, I think I'd have laughed in their face and denied it, but a glance in the mirror confirms the truth. Although the cut on my lip was stitched, there will always be a tiny scar, a reminder of my stupidity.

I understand now how the physical abuse was only a small part of Rob's hold over me. I never admitted it but I was also afraid of other aspects of my life with him. He was controlling, not only with me but also his mother and brother, although I had no ally from those quarters. A dark look from my husband could make me shudder and very often I didn't even know what I'd done wrong. There were days when he refused to speak to me and I ran around in circles trying to placate him. Now I can see the problem was with my husband, not me.

Listening to some of the other women here is amazing. They talk about men who isolated them from their family or friends, making them utterly dependent for food, money and affection. It appears this kind of behaviour has the effect of the victim losing confidence, sometimes to the point of thinking they deserve to be treated in such a way. My case is no different to the others. Even though I had money and plenty of it, I depended on Rob entirely for company, affection and any social life (which was non-existent). What a fool I've been. I knew what he was like from the start but stupidly thought I was in love and hoped my love would change him. Weirdly, this seems to be a recurring theme among my new friends.

So, what's next for me? I can stay here for up to twelve weeks, and the staff will help me find a job and a place to live. Although daunting, it feels exciting too. A new life, perhaps new friends, and a home to call my own.

The police tell me they now have evidence of Rob's involvement with the criminal fraternity in Leeds. When I consented to their search of our home, they took away his computer and found the evidence they needed to charge him, and several of his contacts, with fraud. If I want to press charges of assault, as they're encouraging me to do, together with the cyclist's death all those years ago, they say there's enough to send him away for several years.

I've spoken to Helen a few times on the phone and she's pleased that justice appears to have caught up with Rob. She won't be giving evidence when the trial comes, but the police have her video statement to use and I can verify the details. I was surprised when DC Hamilton told me the extent of Rob's criminal involvement. Having assumed his money was made illegally, I didn't wish to know more but it appeared my husband was tangled up in an *almost* foolproof plan.

A few years ago, Rob became involved with several others who worked out a way to steal diamonds. Rather cunningly, this didn't involve any physical robbery and was done by computers, with the diamonds being delivered to them. Knowing my husband was not particularly good with computers this rather puzzled me, but it seems Rob's role was more of a practical nature. The technical experts worked out a way to hack into the computers of several exclusive jewellers and placed orders, through them, for diamonds. They chose to order from diamond wholesalers in New York and other cities abroad, who would send the stones by secure means to a specified address. If the address was not the regular one the jeweller used with the wholesaler, details of the change and verification from the jeweller were required. The hackers would place the order at night when the shop was closed and intercept the email asking for confirmation of the new address. They then verified it, as if from the jeweller's computer, and the deal was done.

The idea was obviously not my husband's – it was far too complicated and beyond his capabilities. Rob's role was to rent the empty properties used as the delivery address and be there to wait for the parcels. He would sign for them in the jeweller's name and the theft would not be discovered until the wholesaler added the transaction to the jeweller's account, probably at the end of the month, by which time the gang had moved on without a trace.

It was a rather ingenious plan, requiring minimum effort and bringing rich returns. It also involved only a small number of men, whom the police have now arrested, thanks to Rob's computer. Not only did he keep details of the rented houses he'd used but the names and contact details of his partners, presumably to prevent them from cutting him out when dividing the spoils. The same formula was used to undertake several robberies from different jewellers and wholesalers and would most probably have been repeated if the police hadn't curtailed their activities. DC Hamilton told me they'd even found a small diamond in Rob's desk drawer, one they assumed he'd creamed off from a delivery, and one his partners probably knew nothing about. I like to think he planned to get the diamond set and make it into a gift for me, but I'd be kidding myself. Rob only ever cared for himself.

Strangely, I'm relishing the thought of starting a new life and have found a grain of spirit remaining in me which Rob hasn't managed to quash, so the future feels like a positive place to be.

Naturally, I'm happy to help the police, who've been good to me in accepting I knew nothing about these crimes. My husband, too, is apparently talking to them to get a more lenient sentence. However, I will not disclose that I have several thousand pounds from the proceeds of this fraud. I consider this my nest egg, my reward for the years of being Rob's wife. Perhaps in living with Rob for so long, something of his dishonesty has rubbed off onto me.

TWENTY-SEVEN

HELEN

29th November

As I write, the wind outside is blowing fiercely – draughts steal beneath the doors, rattling the windows and eerily moving the curtains. It's turning into one of the worst winters I've known and not only for the weather. My garden looks sadly neglected. James has had neither the time nor decent weather to rake up the last of the autumn leaves. But snow is forecast to arrive soon, hopefully to blanket the garden and hide its sadly neglected state from view.

It's three weeks since that terrible encounter with Rob Wheeler, difficult weeks, both physically and emotionally. I've not ventured far from home, craving the comfort of familiarity. Each day, I've managed to take Gus for at least one walk, and as he is also a lover of home comforts rather than cold rainy weather it's been sufficient for him too. I can feel my strength waning in many ways and I have noticeably lost weight.

What keeps me persevering is the thought of Luke and his family coming home for Christmas. It offers an incentive to make an effort on those mornings when I don't want to get out of bed, and I try to do something each day towards their visit, even if it is only to wrap another present for one of my grandsons. My Christmas shopping has chiefly been courtesy of the internet. Undoubtedly I've been extravagant, almost reckless, enjoying every minute and hopefully my purchases will result in some smiling faces on Christmas morning.

Yesterday, DC Hamilton came to see me with an update on Rob Wheeler's case. From what she told me and from snippets Susan shared during her occasional calls, it seems there's sufficient evidence to bring several charges against Rob. One of these will be a charge of dangerous driving and another of failing to stop after an accident. It almost sounds insignificant when put in such terms, yet the heartache that night caused is anything but. I was pleased to hear he would finally be charged and held accountable, but in the same thought process I wondered how this would impact me. Would I have to give evidence or even face charges myself? Rose Hamilton reassured me on both points.

'We'll not be pressing charges against you, Helen. At the time you were only a child. Rob was the adult and he intimidated you to gain your silence. Coming forward now is of credit to you and not only have you managed to get justice for that incident but several more charges too. You should be proud of yourself! You've been the catalyst in bringing to light other serious crimes for which we have Wheeler and his accomplices. And as for giving evidence, you won't be called for any of the proceedings. We have your video statement, and Susan Wheeler has confirmed your part in the incident. Your health issues have naturally been taken into consideration. I suggest it's time to put this whole debacle behind you and concentrate on enjoying this time with your family. DS Greenwood has asked me to convey his thanks for your help.'

I must have looked incredulous when she spoke those words and Rose smiled, going on to explain, 'Simon's strength isn't with people, so he can appear offhand at times but he's an excellent DS, the best I've ever worked with. He was quite genuine when he asked me to pass on his thanks, we both recognise the tremendous effort you've made in doing this and I for one admire your courage.'

I found it difficult to believe her words and wondered if she was covering for her boss. But that's probably the cynical side of my nature coming through – I should be more trusting. Rose smiled broadly; it must make a change for her to deliver good news when the police so often deal with the sordid side of life. Yet I couldn't feel proud of myself as she suggested and asked, 'Has the man's family been told about these recent developments?'

'Yes, we informed his widow a few days ago that we're bringing charges concerning her husband's death. She was surprised after all this time but pleased nevertheless.'

I wanted to do something more, to apologise, explain, anything which would let her know how sorry I was. A desire I expressed to Rose.

'I understand. What I can do is tell her of the circumstances and your efforts to seek justice. But I don't think you should worry about it. You weren't responsible and when she hears the facts I'm sure she'll understand.'

There was more I wanted to ask, to do, but Rose was probably right – I'd done as much as possible and would have to settle for that.

'What about Susan? Will she lose her house?' It was nothing to do with me but I felt concerned for Susan and didn't wish to see her struggle.

'It's too early to predict what will happen. We're confident Mrs Wheeler knew nothing about her husband's activities therefore won't face charges relating to them but she could lose the property. If Wheeler is convicted and the court feels it appropriate, his assets could be confiscated under the 2002 Proceeds of Crime Act. It will go to the assets recovery agency for civil recovery. Any creditors, such as the insurance company who paid the losses from the jewellery thefts, can claim their money back. As for Susan, I don't think losing the house will worry her. From what I've seen she appears to be enjoying a new life and is making plans for the future. So you see, Helen, things are working themselves out.'

Rose left, surprising me with a hug as she reached the front door. I thanked her for her efforts on my behalf – she'd shown great compassion and I was grateful. Her comments concerning Susan reflected my own thinking on my former friend who'd rung occasionally and appeared to be growing in confidence each time we spoke. She seemed remarkably resilient and enjoyed living in a community and meeting new people and I was pleased for her. Susan's past life hadn't been kind to her – I only hoped the future would be better.

For myself, there's still a pang of regret about the cyclist's widow but perhaps she's also moved on and made a new life for herself. I'm not as satisfied with the results as I'd wanted but can think of nothing else to do. Perhaps it's time for me to move on – it's only a week until Luke, Imogen and Ethan arrive, a comforting thought and I want to savour every moment of their visit. They'll be here for four weeks, taking us into the new year and as this Christmas will be my last, I'm determined to make it one of the best.

Rachel hasn't visited me during the last couple of weeks. A different Macmillan nurse has taken over from her. A lovely young woman called Sarah, who didn't know why there'd been a change. When I asked, she promised to try and find out for me but no more has been said and I don't want to push the issue. As far as Sarah knew, Rachel was not ill, so the change was somewhat perplexing.

Sarah suggested introducing opioid medication as the pain was increasing, but I had my own timetable and didn't wish to consider this until after Christmas. Instead, we compromised by increasing the Naprosyn and other painkillers which I trusted would dull the pain. The cancer symptoms are certainly making themselves felt, with uncomfortable bloating accompanying the pain. In addition, I seem plagued with fatigue lately and regularly sleep for a couple of hours each afternoon which helps a little and my focus is on getting through Christmas, after which, who knows? It may then be time to let Gus go to Megan. I'll miss him terribly but will see him often when I visit them.

6th December

The fields were covered with a light dusting of snow this morning, which added to the brightness of the day, creating a dazzling white landscape which I longed to capture in my mind and remember in days to come. I drove to the edge of town with Gus to let him run over the common and hopefully exhaust himself in so doing. Later today, my son will be arriving from Canada and the excitement almost makes me squeal. They land at Heathrow this morning and pick up a hire car to drive north, arriving by teatime. I know they'll be tired after such a long flight, particularly Ethan who's never flown before. To have them here with me will be so wonderful – I can hardly wait!

Over the last week or so, I've experienced a terrible sense of foreboding, at times convincing myself I would die before Luke arrived. But I'm still here and it's only a matter of hours until I see them all again. So perhaps my prayers were heard after all.

TWENTY-EIGHT

RACHEL

I'm ashamed to say I've done something I've never resorted to before in my career – to stop seeing a patient because I no longer felt the compassion towards her which I should.

It's four weeks since my last visit to Helen Reid when her disclosure left me so shaken I just had to leave her home. Yes, I feel regret now, but more disappointment in myself and the unprofessional manner we parted. The telephone call she took during our last visit allowed me to leave before I said something I might later regret.

After my abrupt exit I went straight to the office and arranged for a colleague to take on Helen as a patient without any explanation. If my colleague thought it unusual, she didn't comment – it's acknowledged and generally accepted that there are times when a patient is transferred to another nurse's list, although it rarely happens. When it does it's generally assumed the relationship with the patient is not working out or there's something which touches us too personally to be able to offer our very best. In this case my judgement that the change was better for all concerned was accepted without question and Helen Reid was passed on to a colleague, Sarah.

Until the day of my last visit I'd have described our relationship as good. I liked Helen and think the feeling was mutual, although there was always something there, something she seemed to want to tell me yet couldn't verbalise for some reason. Her words hit me like a physical blow when she eventually confided in me.

At the beginning of her story, I didn't understand exactly what she was saying – Helen seemed confused and as people often do, assumed I knew the background to her story, even though her telling of it was disjointed. In trying to understand and put myself in her shoes, I asked who the 'poor man' was to whom she referred.

We were interrupted at that point by the telephone and as Helen answered the call she hurriedly said, 'The cyclist killed that night by Rob's car.'

It was the moment I realised... when the shock of her words hit me head-on and I connected her story to the terrible night a hit-and-run driver killed my father. The realisation left me completely drained and as I walked out of the house and automatically climbed into my car, I was trembling. It was several minutes before I was able to drive.

Helen Reid was in the car which killed my father all those years ago; she witnessed his death first-hand and did nothing about it!

I believe Helen rang the office after my hasty retreat but left no message and I should have returned the call but couldn't bring myself to do so. She also rang a week later when again I made no attempt to return her call. I wouldn't have known what to say. After that, Helen appeared to accept my replacement and didn't attempt to contact me again.

My mum rarely talked about my father's death, which isn't to say she doesn't talk about him but I only remember the things she's told me over the years about the man, not his demise. She painted beautiful, detailed word pictures for me, making me feel as if I'd actually known him and even remembered him, which is impossible – when Dad was killed my mother was in the early stages of pregnancy and neither of my parents knew I was on the way.

Mum always said I kept her going, that I was a part of him given as a precious gift to comfort her. I cannot remember even one expression of bitterness at what happened although she loved her husband dearly. I knew a hit-and-run driver killed Dad and as I grew older I think I felt more anger at the circumstances than Mum did. This faceless, nameless figure robbed me of a father, and now there was a connection with Helen Reid.

My initial anger transferred to her, although precisely what involvement she had in the events of the night I was unsure – I left without giving Helen a chance to explain. It was a cruel night which robbed me of any opportunity to know my father and made my mother a widow. Typically, my mother, Martha Walters, did what she's done for the whole of her life and looked for the silver lining, which in this case happened to be me.

Having learned something of the circumstances which had always been a mystery, I agonised over whether to tell Mum about Helen Reid, weighing the case for and against without reaching a conclusion. I shared my turmoil with Ben, who as he always does, listened sagely before telling me it was a decision only I could make. I found myself wondering about the events of that night, tearing myself up inside as I imagined images of my poor father left to die alone at the roadside. Questions rattled in my brain, keeping me awake at night. Was Helen, or the driver, drunk? Did they feel remorse at what they'd done, and did my father die instantly or suffer pain?

Since learning of Helen's involvement, I've looked again at photographs of my father. I have copies of all the ones Mum has, the formal posed wedding day images and the more relaxed newlyweds' snapshots. Each one almost screams out their happiness and love, so touching yet heartbreakingly poignant.

As it happened, the decision to tell Mum was taken out of my hands. One morning, she arrived a little early to look after the girls and asked if I had time to talk before work. There was no time to ponder over what she might want as Mum came straight out and told me the police had been in contact and were charging someone in connection with Dad's death. Her words were measured and even, and knowing her as well as I know myself, I realised she'd carefully considered each word to make the news as palatable as possible. True to form, my mother thought about me rather than herself even though she suffered all the heartache at the time. I asked how she felt about it and her reply was typical.

'I'm pleased they've eventually found the man who did this but don't you think he'll have suffered enough by carrying the guilt of what he did over all these years?' Mum always chose to look for the good in people. I was stunned and couldn't form an answer. There was no sure way of knowing if the perpetrator experienced remorse, or was there? It was my turn to talk, but my dilemma was in breaching patient confidentiality if I told Mum about Helen. I could explain how a patient had some involvement and leave *the patient* vaguely anonymous but would it benefit anyone?

I remained silent. Mum appeared to be handling this unexpected news well, and what could I add to anything the police had told her? The answer was nothing. I'd listened to Helen Reid pouring out her angst about an incident from years ago but hadn't stayed to hear the end of the story. After considering the very little I did know and doing the maths, it appeared Helen would have been about sixteen years old at the time – still only a child.

What had I done? Helen didn't have a chance to finish the story before I left, leaving her to wonder what had caused me to run away and subsequently ignore her for so long.

I hugged my mother before kissing Charlotte and Katy and leaving for work. Mum's words resonated in my mind – her readiness to forgive the driver whom she assumed would have received punishment enough by his guilt. Martha Walters was undoubtedly one of the most kind-hearted people I've ever known. But should I take her lead and try to forgive? I knew I must, my upbringing had instilled some of the goodness of my parents in me and I was in no doubt I'd treated Helen shabbily and would not settle until I apologised.

TWENTY-NINE
HELEN

7th December

I have no words to describe how wonderful it is to have my family around me. My excitement when they arrived yesterday equalled Ethan's. There was no shyness from my grandson this time! Luke hugged me gently, then holding my shoulders, looked closely at me, frowning at what he saw. I could almost read his thoughts as I could when he was a little boy and said, 'I know, there's not as much of me now. I'm aiming for the supermodel waifish look!' He smiled knowingly and moved away to let me hug Imogen. It was brilliant to see them again. We spent the evening chatting about anything and everything. Megan, James and Sam came over with fish and chips for all, which the travellers ate with gusto.

I can't remember when Megan and James left, but it wasn't easy to persuade Sam to go home when he'd made a new friend in his cousin. They would be back tomorrow, fresher after a good night's sleep.

When I awoke this morning, it was to the usual moment of uncertainty, not knowing what day it was or what I needed to do. But when I heard movement in the kitchen below, yesterday's events came flooding back and I smiled, eager to join my family. Imogen had made herself at home as I'd told her to and was making breakfast. Ethan jumped up to hug me, almost knocking me over and earning a rebuke from his father.

'Please don't stop him – I don't want to be treated like a china doll. I love his exuberance!'

'Okay.' Luke smiled and joined in the hug, enfolding me in his strong embrace where I wished I could remain forever. My ordinarily quiet house was full of chatter and laughter, precisely how I wanted it to be. Sitting at the table, I let Imogen pour me tea and put bread in the toaster; the days of serving them were regrettably over but I was content to allow my daughter-in-law to fuss.

'We've taken Gus for his walk,' Ethan chirped, which explained why my dog was fast asleep in his basket.

'Oh, thank you. You must have been up early?'

Luke sighed. 'Our sleeping patterns are all haywire. I've been awake since five thirty, and Ethan woke soon after, so we thought we'd take Gus on a long walk.'

'He'll certainly have enjoyed that; I can't take him as far as I used to. Now, what are the plans for today?'

'Well, Megan's working today so I wondered if you'd like me to take you to see Gran? I want to visit a few times while I'm here so if you're up to it we can go today.'

'Yes, today's as good as any but you'll see a big difference in her. Your gran rarely knows who I am and can be quite rude when the mood takes her. She's settling down after a difficult spell of being aggressive towards the staff and other residents. The doctor changed her medication which seems to have calmed her down somewhat, but it also makes her rather sleepy.'

'Perhaps just you and I should go; Imogen, will you be okay with Ethan for a couple of hours?' Luke asked.

'Of course, we can wrap up and go to the park, can't we, Ethan?'

It was settled and within an hour Luke and I were on our way to The Valley. The early morning frost had given way to bright sunshine, although the temperature was only slightly above freezing. Trees lined the sides of the road, bare and solemn. Winter had taken its icy grip and where I would generally anticipate the coming spring, I wished time would stand still for once.

It was a relief to have Luke at the wheel. It's time for me to give up driving altogether, as there are fewer places I feel up to going to and I'd hate to be the cause of an accident. I've been there before...

The Valley's garden was closed for winter, flowerbeds dug over and mulched, with more bare trees at each side of the drive, their gnarled black branches seeming to form a guard of honour as we approached the home. Having prepared Luke for the shock of seeing how much his grandmother had deteriorated, I was worried about the reaction we would get from her. It was at least three years since Luke last visited and Mum would almost certainly not remember him.

After parking in the designated area, we crunched over the gravel on our way to the main entrance. Being a Victorian building, The Valley had similarities to the hospice, a place with which I was becoming familiar. The red brick, in good repair, was recently repointed and the windows appeared to be the original sash ones, sanded and painted in white gloss which stood out against the darkness of the day. Inside, a high entrance hall offered four different directions to choose from and after signing in I turned to the one which led to the communal lounge. Luke followed, taking in the surroundings with a frown. Inevitably these homes have a distinctive smell, masked here by floral air freshener but still discernible. I smiled at my son and took his arm as we approached the lounge.

As always, the television was on yet only a few residents were paying attention to it. Mum was in a wheelchair at the far side of the room. Luke would probably not have recognised her himself. She was asleep, oblivious to the noise of the television, chin on her chest and arms flopped down into her lap with palms facing upwards as if waiting for a gift. Gently, I took her hand and spoke to her, waiting for the slow process of waking up. As her head lifted, Mum looked straight at us without any recognition. I began pushing her from the lounge to her room, where we could have more privacy. She made no comment until we sat on the edge of the bed facing this shrunken old lady who used to be my strong, vivacious mother.

'Is he with you?' she growled. I nodded.

'It's Luke, Mum, your grandson, remember?' She clearly didn't and glared at us both from beneath scowling eyebrows. I started the usual monologue, this time with more to say about Luke, Imogen and Ethan. From my bag I retrieved a small book of photographs, aptly called 'Grandma's Boasting Book', and showed her the images, reciting the names of her family who used to be the centre of her universe. Mum sat silently, paying no attention to the photographs and glancing from me to Luke.

'And who are you?' she asked me with a look of disgust on her face. Although she'd asked this or a similar question many times in recent months, the words, coupled with how she spoke them, hit me forcibly. Suddenly it was all too much. Tears welled in my eyes and as Luke squeezed my hand, I stood, apologising and left the room. Leaning on the wall a couple of doors down I listened as Luke picked up the one-sided conversation, speaking gently to his grandmother, telling her how much he – we all, loved her. When I heard him begin a sentence with, 'Do you remember...' I hurried down the corridor to the matron's office. She smiled as I approached then came closer when she saw the tears. Her arms surrounded me and I sobbed like a baby as she stroked my hair. When I managed to pull myself together, the matron steered me to a chair and halted my apologies.

'Helen, there's no need to say sorry. You have so much going on in your life at present and I find it remarkable how you still visit your mother, particularly the way she is.'

I blew my nose and told her my son from Canada was with me. The matron nodded and then I told her the decision I'd only just made.

'I think I shall make this my last visit to Mum.'

The matron nodded, her faint smile reassuring, concurring with my decision.

'I'm going to have to give up the car, driving's getting too much for me and I don't want to rely on other people all the time. So, I shall say my goodbyes today.'

As the matron studied me, she seemed aware of how much I'd changed too. My weight loss was noticeable, with clothes so poorly fitting that only my bloated stomach kept them from dropping off altogether. Very little flesh was left on my face, and I avoided looking in the mirror these days, not wanting to see the haggard old woman with sunken cheeks staring back at me. My collarbones were so prominent that I'd taken to wearing scarves all the time.

'That's a wise decision, Helen. To be candid, your mother doesn't recognise anyone now, and it obviously causes you pain to see her so altered. The mother you knew and loved left us a long time ago,' the matron said kindly. I stood to thank her and returned to Mum's room. Luke held her hand, still talking while she gazed out the window as if no one else was in the room. Quietly I told Luke of my decision. He smiled his understanding and tactfully said he would wait in the lobby.

I picked up Mum's hairbrush and ran it through her hair like she had done countless times for me as a child. Still, there was no response to what I hoped would be a soothing, intimate gesture. I knelt before her and took both of her hands in mine. They felt cold despite the room's warmth and I rubbed them gently.

'Mum, I'm going now... and I shan't be coming back. I'm not well and won't be here much longer. Megan will still come, and Luke will come again before he goes home to Canada. I love you, Mum.' I kissed her cheek – the papery translucent skin felt soft and smelled of talcum powder. She lifted her watery blue eyes to meet mine for a moment, and I thought she understood, but she was gone again in an instant. I looked at my mother for one last time then turned to leave.

Luke was talking to the matron when I found him. He pulled me into his strong body and put a protective arm around my shoulders. We said goodbye to the matron. I wanted to express my thanks but couldn't speak. She understood and gently squeezed my arm as we left.

A pensive silence filled the car on the way home. Luke somehow understood that I needed to think and put a CD in the player, an unfamiliar tune but one with a gentle, soothing melody. I couldn't help comparing my mother's situation to my own. It was impossible to say which of us had the better deal: Mum, whose mind had failed, or me, whose body was letting me down.

THIRTY

HELEN

10th December

We quickly slipped into a comfortable routine, with Luke, Imogen and Ethan having breakfast with me, and then lunch and dinner with Megan. Unfortunately, this morning I'd not gone with them. My body screamed at me again after not sleeping well because of the pain. It's perhaps time to concede to taking a more potent opioid-based drug, which I'd not wanted to do until after Christmas. But I fear this pain will prevent me from enjoying the traditional family celebrations I was looking forward to.

The doorbell rang as I sat in the lounge, stroking Gus's silky ears and reading the last chapter of a novel I'd been enjoying. Rachel Amos stood on my step and I moved aside to let her in. I was pleased to see her and told her so. I'd often thought about her and wondered why our relationship ended so abruptly. It appears I was about to find out.

Rachel politely declined an offer of coffee, saying she didn't have much time – and then the bombshell dropped. 'I must apologise for the way I left so hurriedly without an explanation.' Her words were measured and sounded melancholy, unusual for her, but after a moment she continued. 'When you told me of your quest to put right a wrong from the past, it didn't connect with me until you mentioned a cyclist who'd been killed. The cyclist was my father.'

To say there was a stunned silence would be the understatement of the decade. I could hardly believe what Rachel told me and my heart pounded rapidly. I shuffled uncomfortably on the sofa, avoiding eye contact, suddenly ashamed and appalled with myself. My visitor spoke first.

'It was wrong of me to leave without an explanation. I can only say it was the shock – I didn't know what to say or do.'

'I understand.' My brain struggled to grasp what Rachel had just told me. 'Er, are you sure this was the same accident?' I pathetically managed to blurt out.

'The twentieth of October 1970?' she said, leaving no doubt it was her father lying dead on the road on that fateful night. The image of his still, lifeless body once again came to mind, a picture which had haunted me throughout my teens and adult life.

'Oh, Rachel, I am so terribly sorry!' It was incredible and brought the incident into a completely different perspective as I looked at the woman who'd been denied the presence and love of a father because of that horrendous night. I didn't know what to say and neither it seemed, did she. I wanted to do something practical but this wasn't a situation where that kind of help was appropriate, and besides, my capabilities were diminishing every day.

'Maybe we can have a coffee now. Shall I make it?' Rachel recognised my anxiety and her training came into play. Nodding my permission, I sank back into the sofa and took a few deep breaths, glad to be alone for a few minutes to try and understand the implications of Rachel's revelation. Was there something I could do or say to this poor young woman?

Needless to say, nothing came to mind. My heart was racing, so much so I could feel the pulse throbbing in my neck. My face was flushed with shame and embarrassment. I tried to speak when Rachel returned to the room but the words wouldn't flow. My visitor sat in a chair opposite, passed me a coffee and looked directly at me.

'When you told me about your recent visits to the police, which were connected to the past, you were rather vague and it didn't register with me just how long ago it was. Then, when you mentioned the man on the bike, your story started to make sense. I was shocked, and when the phone rang, I left without allowing you to explain properly. Would you tell me more about it now? I'd like to understand your role in this.' Rachel was handing me a lifeline, a chance to present my version of events. Taking a deep breath, I took the chance to try to explain.

'I was barely more than a child and besotted with Rob Wheeler even though he had a *bad boy* reputation. We met secretly, knowing my parents would never approve, and my friend Susan covered for me. Rob often used his brother's car and was showing off by going far too fast – and I think he'd been drinking. It was dusk, the light was fading and he didn't see the cyclist, your father, as he turned the corner. By then it was too late. The car hit him full-on then careered into the side of the road and stopped. As I tried to get out to see if I could help, Rob dragged me back inside and pulled away. He ignored my pleas to stop and when he took me home, he hit me and threatened me to gain my silence. It was all so frightening.'

I paused to catch my breath; this was one of the most difficult conversations of my life. Rachel waited silently for me to continue.

'I heard the next day that your father had died and didn't know what to do. Rob wasn't the kind of person to cross and I was scared, aware of his reputation. Since then I've loathed myself for being so weak. As the days passed it became harder to tell anyone the truth, and when we moved away from the area shortly afterwards I tried to forget it ever happened. But of course, I couldn't. It's haunted and shamed me for all these years. If I could turn the clock back without hesitation, I would.'

'And this is what you've been trying to do – put right this wrong from your past?' Rachel's voice was barely a whisper. Hearing the stark details of her father's death can't have been easy.

'Yes, but even now I'm unsure if going to the police was the right thing to do. I saw Rob first to allow him to own up to his crime which was useless. He was never going to admit to it. Yet the police seem happy enough now because Rob was already known to them, and the incident with the gun gave them the opportunity to search his house and find evidence of his other criminal activities.

'My original intention wasn't to get him into trouble but to somehow bring a sense of peace to your mother. Perhaps this is something which can't ever happen, which makes me wonder if it's all been worthwhile.'

Rachel was shaking her head. 'Oh, Helen, you've been beating yourself up all this time and you're not up to it. Just look at you.' My appearance must have altered in the weeks since we'd last met. I knew I was failing, and with Rachel's visit, I felt even worse as it brought home to me just what she and her mother must have suffered during the intervening years.

'Did your mother ever remarry?' It was none of my business, but if she'd gone on to lead a happy life with someone else, it might make me feel a little better.

'No, she never remarried. My parents had only been married for five months when Dad died and Mum wasn't interested in anyone else. We became very close, the two of us, living for each other I suppose, and even today we remain close and the girls think the world of her.'

'She must really hate me?' I had to ask, didn't I?

'I doubt it. My mother's never hated anyone in her life. When the police told her they'd arrested someone for Dad's death, she almost seemed sympathetic, assuming whoever it was must have been living with guilt all this time.'

'Your mother sounds like a remarkable woman. I did ask the police to tell her how sorry I was. Do you know if they passed my message on?'

'If they did she never mentioned it.'

Rachel's reaction was difficult to judge. Coming to visit me demonstrated a degree of forgiveness. She clearly hadn't come to berate me and genuinely appeared to want to understand. I still desperately needed to try to put this right and if I could meet her mother to offer my apologies, perhaps this was my opportunity to do so.

'Do you think your mother would agree to meet me so I can apologise in person?'

Rachel's eyes widened; she considered the request for a moment before asking, 'Are you up to a meeting, Helen? Reliving the past has been traumatic for you and you're far from well. Can you not let this drop now?'

'I knew it wouldn't be easy when I began, but going to the police was all I could do. I'm only grateful they didn't charge me as an accomplice. As it stands, I'm not sure I've done enough. Perhaps meeting your mother to tell her how sorry I am will help us both.'

'I'll have to think about it. Mum knows nothing about you – to tell her would have breached our nurse/patient confidentiality so I'd need your permission to disclose how we met. Would that be okay?'

'Yes, that's fine. Your mother must be a remarkable lady and she's certainly raised you well.'

The conversation dried up – our relationship could never return to what it was before. Finally, after agreeing to consider arranging a meeting, Rachel left. Feeling drained by the unexpected visit I dozed for the rest of the morning on the sofa, almost in a trance and seeing in my mind's eye the picture of a young newlywed girl being told the devastating news that her husband was dead.

In a way Rachel's visit felt as if I'd been given one last chance to lay this whole sorry mess to rest. I only hoped she would ask her mother for the opportunity to apologise and that this lady was as generous in spirit as her daughter was.

THIRTY-ONE

HELEN

17th December

Having heard nothing from Rachel for a week, any meeting with her mother seemed unlikely. It was a huge disappointment but I determinedly refused to get hung up on this to the exclusion of everything else. There simply wasn't time. With my family close at hand and Christmas swiftly approaching, each day held plenty of distractions. Ethan and Luke were proving to be a delight. They'd been told I was unwell and they mustn't make too many demands on me, which to their credit, they didn't, but their presence lifted my spirit. I became adept at so many board games which I'd never even heard of previously and mastered the art of losing at Snap without the boys knowing it was fixed.

Naturally, the boys' excitement grew as Christmas approached and they hated being apart. Ethan was sleeping at Megan's now more often than at my house with his parents, but seeing their bond growing so strong was good. With my body failing me slightly more each day, I found it challenging to keep up with many of the activities planned with the children in mind and occasionally I was glad of a few quiet hours to myself, so I encouraged them to enjoy their time together. One of the exceptions to this was when the boys were going to see Father Christmas in one of the big department stores in Manchester. It was also the first time I agreed to use the newly acquired wheelchair, which Luke insisted on buying, knowing I was almost housebound without it as walking had become so painful.

On the morning in question, when I was ready to leave, I caught a glimpse of myself in the cheval mirror in my room and it seemed as if a gaunt stranger was looking back at me. My skin was sallow with a translucent quality which aged me considerably. I'd lost weight but was bloated in my abdomen and legs, resulting in an unbalanced look over my whole body. On the positive side, the bloating was the only thing keeping my trousers up and I certainly didn't want the bother of buying new clothes. However, my reflection shocked me – the cancer had ravaged my body in a relatively short time, visibly taking its toll. I moved away from the mirror, vowing to close my eyes in future when I passed it, or better still, give the mirror away. Perhaps I should take a leaf out of Claire the masseuse's book and be a little more creative with make-up to brighten my appearance.

We took two cars, Megan, James and the boys in their car and me, Imogen and Luke in the hired car. Having managed to keep together for most of the journey, we eventually found a couple of spaces in a multi-storey car park with a lift down to the shops. The city centre was buzzing, full of Christmas shoppers eager to spend their money and be dazzled by the fantastic displays in the shop windows. I was gratified to see the store we were visiting first still displayed a traditional nativity scene; a stable with Mary, Joseph and baby Jesus. Animals, shepherds and wise men completed the tableau where we stood for several minutes, considering what Christmas actually means. *Jesus is the reason for the season.* I remember my mother displaying a poster with those words in pride of place among our decorations. The boys were eager to visit Father Christmas, and as we knew it would be impossible to do anything else until they'd seen the big man himself, we made it our first stop.

Santa's grotto was magical, with abundant fairy lights, elves to entertain the waiting children and a golden glittering carpet which disappeared through an ivy-decked tunnel into a darkened room. Ethan and Sam suddenly became very self-conscious, shyly dropping their heads when an elf attempted to engage them in conversation while waiting in the queue. Wide-eyed, they took in the elaborate decorations and the enormous, magnificent tree festooned with lights and baubles. When their turn came to be ushered inside, the adults following on behind, our anticipation almost equalled the children's. Once within, the grotto did not disappoint. A relatively small space was transformed into an enchanting cave with even more fairy lights, brightly decorated miniature trees, and bells gently tinkling. We took in the atmosphere in a moment of silence. Mechanical elves were busy making toys in one corner while a full-sized toy reindeer lay curled up on a bed of straw in another.

Ethan and Sam moved shyly towards a jolly Father Christmas who slapped his knee and said, 'Ho, ho!' He was an excellent Santa, resplendent in a thick red robe with white fur trimmings; his shoulders sprinkled with glittering snow to add to the enchantment. The boys appeared so small and timid in his presence yet managed to whisper what they would like for Christmas and remembered to say 'thank you' for the presents received from the big man himself.

As they stood close to Father Christmas an elf appeared with a camera. My grandsons' smiles were rather forced, all previous bravado disappearing as they shyly posed for the photograph. The captivating scene filled my heart with love and knowing I'd never experience another Christmas, I felt truly blessed to share in this one.

The bright lights momentarily dazzled me as we moved out of the grotto. I blinked to clear my blurred vision and only then realised there were tears in my eyes. Next, we spent an inordinate amount of time in the toy department, where the boys became enthusiastic quality-testers of all the latest new toys. It was a relief to see their passion for some of the things I'd already purchased for them and hidden away at Megan's house. Here too, the Christmas decorations were amazing and as I watched my grandsons check out the tree, their two fair heads close together whispering childish secrets, I was reminded of Luke and Megan at a similar age. The close relationship growing between the boys delighted me and I dearly hoped their parents would find a way to nurture their friendship as they grew up on opposite sides of the world.

It proved almost impossible to drag the boys away from the toy department, so James offered to stay a while longer while the rest of us went in search of the store café for refreshments. Imogen insisted on staying too, perhaps a diplomatic ploy to allow me time alone with my children? Whatever, it was wonderful to be with all my family. Knowing your time is limited focuses the mind and forces you to rethink your priorities.

Our wander around the shops after coffee was not in search of gifts; we were all well-prepared for Christmas and so browsed, taking in the atmosphere and enjoying the bustling mood of other shoppers as they thanked sales staff and wished them a merry Christmas. The only last-minute shopping for us would be fresh fruit and vegetables for Christmas dinner. I was a little saddened this year at being unable to cook for the family, but the presence of Luke, Imogen and Ethan certainly made up for any disappointment and I could provide mince pies and other goodies from my well-stocked freezer.

The day was declared a success; we'd been leisurely in our meandering, with the unequivocal highlight being the visit to Father Christmas. The boys talked non-stop about it, their bravado telling the tale much more than the actual event. On our return to Megan's home, the children settled to watch a Disney DVD while the adults enjoyed tea and much-needed rest.

THIRTY-TWO
RACHEL

Four weddings and a funeral are not the usual order of things in my line of work. Four funerals and a wedding is the ratio I'm used to, and today I attended another funeral. I don't go to all my patients' farewell services but this was for a courageous young woman who, at twenty-three years old, was stricken with breast cancer. Stacey was an inspiration who battled on after a double mastectomy and what must have seemed like endless chemotherapy treatments, sadly all to no avail.

Stacey lost her hair and joked about it, frequently removing her wig in the most unlikely places to scratch her scalp. Once she did so in a restaurant, embarrassing her mother as she ate dessert with her blond wig hanging off the seat beside her. After losing her hair, Stacey had an intricate and rather large tattoo of a butterfly on the back of her head, and if people looked twice at her, she asked them if they liked her 'scalp art' – they usually ended up smiling at this young woman's bravery.

The service this morning was typical of her spirit. The coffin was brought into the crematorium as the song, 'Lady in Red', played, and she'd requested all mourners to wear bright colours, strictly no black. Stacey had even written her eulogy, which was read aloud by a close friend – her humour and pragmatic attitude were the dominant themes of the service. Attending a funeral often teaches me much more about a person than I learned in my brief acquaintance with them. There were inevitable tears from Stacey's family, although they tried to be brave as their daughter wished, and everything considered if Stacey had been watching, I'm sure she'd have approved of the whole thing.

Sitting at the back of the room, my thoughts drifted to my father's funeral. Having not been born and as my mother rarely talked about the event, I didn't know if there'd been a church service or a simple ceremony here at the crematorium. Dad would have been about the same age as Stacey – a life suddenly cut short when he should have been planning his future as a newly married man. It was even more tragic as he was unaware that he was to become a father. And what about Mum? I've always known her as a strong and capable woman, but was that due to being left to face motherhood alone? Undoubtedly there'd have been tears at my father's funeral and in the weeks and months afterwards, but I knew so little about those early years and my mother's struggle to support and care for a baby alone. My childhood recollections started like most people's memories do, from about three or four years old, the years before then are a complete mystery.

Still undecided about whether to tell Mum about Helen Reid, I could see possible advantages for both women, particularly Helen, who needed a sense of peace in these last weeks of her life. Yet my mother remained my chief concern. Would meeting the woman who was there at Dad's death and knew what occurred that night benefit or distress her?

After the police informed Mum of Rob Wheeler's arrest, and since the morning she told me, the subject hadn't been mentioned between us, although I'm sure it must be on her mind. My dilemma is whether a meeting of these two women, connected by this historic crime, is prudent. Would learning that the driver had been drinking and refused to stop and help distress Mum? Would telling her story give Helen the peace she craves? It was impossible to predict the answers to these questions. I wanted Helen to find peace, but not at my mother's expense – yet did I have the right to decide for either of them?

As Stacey's funeral ended, I filed out of the crematorium behind the family and other mourners to shake hands with her parents. They thanked me for helping their daughter, which I brushed aside as simply doing my job. However, they insisted on telling me how much my involvement had helped Stacey prepare for the end of her life. Again, I felt humbled as I left them in the garden of remembrance among dozens of floral tributes to their daughter, and again my thoughts turned to Helen Reid. This was the moment I decided to tell Mum about Helen and let her decide if she wished to meet her.

Arriving back from the crematorium, my home embraced me with its warmth and comfort. Mum usually fed the children before Ben and I were home and generally prepared something for us to eat. She seemed her usual chirpy self, and I almost backed out of my resolve, again trying to foretell how such a meeting would work out for her. I introduced the topic with a question. 'Have you heard any more from the police, Mum?'

'No, it's still early days yet – the legal process can take forever – but they'll be in touch when they have something to tell me.'

'It's just – I have a patient who was involved in Dad's death – but only in a small way...'

I suddenly had Mum's full attention, my words an obvious shock.

'What do you mean, involved?'

'Her name is Helen, and she was a passenger in the car

which hit Dad. She tried to get the driver to stop but he wouldn't and she's regretted it ever since.'

'Why didn't she go to the police?' Mum looked unusually pale. I faltered, wondering if I'd done the right thing in telling her.

'She was only sixteen, and the driver threatened her.'

'And you say she's a patient? She has cancer then, is it terminal?'

'Yes. Helen's been trying to put this right since her diagnosis. It's due to her visit to the police that they arrested this man. Helen would like to meet you, to apologise in person – but you don't have to if it would be painful, I can tell her no.'

My mother looked thoughtful, slightly frowning as she considered my words, but only briefly.

'Yes, I'll meet her. Fix it up to suit your patient – you know which times will suit me.' And the subject was closed for the time being.

THIRTY-THREE

HELEN

18th December

The telephone woke me from a restless sleep but was answered before I could pull myself together. Luke quietly poked his head around the door of my room and I smiled at my handsome son.

'There's a lady on the phone for you, Rachel, I think her name is. Shall I ask her to ring back later?'

I was suddenly wide awake. 'No, it's okay, bring me the phone and I'll speak to her now.'

Luke brought the telephone to the bed and left the room to give me some privacy.

'Sorry to wake you, Helen. How are you feeling today?' Rachel's familiar voice sounded the same as ever, but I didn't want to engage in small talk when my heart was pounding in anticipation.

'I'm fine, thank you. Did you speak to your mother?'

'Yes. Mum was surprised, obviously, but she's agreed to meet you if we can fix a suitable time. Is it too near Christmas for you now? Would you rather leave it until after the holiday?'

'No, please, can we make it soon? I can get a taxi if you tell me when and where.' I was painfully aware if we left it until after Christmas it might be too late, and besides, this was a meeting I'd waited so long for.

'I think it would be better for us to visit you, Helen. Travelling in your condition's not a good idea, especially in this weather. Would later this afternoon be too soon for you?'

I was stunned at such generosity and today was as good as any so I accepted Rachel's offer. We disconnected somewhat awkwardly. I slid my legs out of bed and stood up to prepare for the day ahead, more than a little apprehensive about how it would work out.

Telling Luke my nurse was visiting later today and I needed a quiet day at home, he suggested that as they were going to buy the tree this morning, they'd take it straight to Megan's then come to pick me up after my visitor left – I'd ring him when I was ready.

An hour later, after Luke, Imogen and Sam went out for the day, I ran a deep bath, added some of my favourite bath salts and relaxed in the hot water, attempting to calm my body and my mind. It was quiet downstairs and I was simultaneously relieved and saddened to be alone. My mind raced with scenarios of what might happen later in the afternoon – should I make coffee – would there be small talk? It was possibly the most surreal situation I'd ever been in and the morning dragged on relentlessly. I tried reading, listening to relaxing music, and even eating chocolate when I couldn't face a meal, but nothing calmed me like I hoped it would.

At two o'clock the front doorbell chimed. Gus pricked up his ears and thumped his tail on the carpet at the prospect of visitors whilst I tried to swallow the huge lump in my throat.

Martha Walters was not what I expected and certainly nothing like her daughter. She was small whereas Rachel was tall with red hair. Rachel must take after her father. In Martha's face I saw compassion rather than the hostility and accusing demeanour I'd expected and felt I deserved. She held out her hand which I tentatively took. There was an aura about this woman, a serenity I'd never managed to achieve in my own life. Her hand felt small and warm as she held mine for a moment or two, looking at me as if sizing me up, but with a smile which went some way to relax my tense body. I asked my visitors to sit down and offered coffee. Rachel accepted on the condition she could make it. Nodding my agreement, I was left alone with the woman I'd wanted, yet dreaded, to meet.

Martha sat on the sofa, with me on the armchair gripping my hands together to stop the trembling sensation which had overtaken me. Is there a protocol for such a situation? It was up to me to speak first but the words I'd rehearsed in my mind all day long now seemed shallow and inadequate. What do you say to a woman whose husband had been killed – a crime in which you were complicit? There was no precedent for such an occasion as this but I was rescued from my inadequacies when Martha Walters opened the conversation.

'I'm sorry to hear about your illness – it must be difficult for you.' Her voice was gentle, the words full of compassion. I nodded. Saying thank you seemed inappropriate.

Knowing it was up to me to bring up the reason for our meeting, I forced myself to speak. 'Mrs Walters, I can't tell you how sorry I am for not coming forward after your husband's death. It was very wrong of me, unforgivable, and something I've always regretted. I know that nothing I say will make it right, but I truly am sorry.' As the words left my mouth they sounded bland – ineffective and insufficient, yet what else could I say or do.

'From what Rachel tells me it appears you've lived with the guilt of that night for all these years, but I've never blamed you. Yes, I was angry at the driver for not stopping, but the hospital said Michael probably died instantly – upon impact and didn't suffer. And we didn't know someone else was in the car until you came forward. It was a courageous thing to do, and I suppose I've come here today hoping to find out exactly what happened. Are you up to telling me, Helen?'

Why isn't this lady angry with me?

Recalling the worst evening of my life and probably Martha's too was painful but the least I could do, so haltingly, I looked at this woman who I'd wronged and told her what she'd asked.

'I was sixteen and Rob was much older. We were out in his brother's car for the evening, and he was driving recklessly. I'm pretty sure he'd been drinking too. Rob didn't see your husband until we hit him – it was on a bend he took far too quickly. After the impact the car swerved off the road and stopped. I tried to leave the car, to see if there was anything I could do, but Rob wouldn't let me. He started the car again, dragged me back inside and sped away.

'I know it was weak of me to go along with what he said, inexcusable – but I was shocked. When we arrived back in Grimethorpe, Rob hit me and left me in no doubt that I was to keep quiet. I was so afraid of him and unable to face my parents so I went to a friend's house. She suggested going to the police, which I knew was the right thing to do, but I was paralysed by fear and to my shame and regret said nothing. The next morning when I heard of your husband's death, I should have told my parents and the police but fear held me back and again I did nothing.'

Rachel returned to the lounge with coffee and we paused to take the mugs from the tray, giving me a chance to think of anything else I should add which might help them understand. Nothing came to mind, but I didn't want to sit there trying to make my part in the incident look any less than it was. The temptation was to play on my fear of Rob, to blame him entirely when I was also culpable even if it was to a lesser degree.

'I've told you how frightened I was of Rob but it's no excuse for what I did or didn't do that evening and I know nothing I say will make it any better for you. If I could turn the clock back, I would – I'm so very, very sorry.' While speaking, I forced myself to maintain eye contact with Martha, which was far from easy. She appeared eager to hear my story and had so far listened quietly. As my words dried up, I waited for a reaction from her or Rachel, preparing myself for the worst.

'Helen,' Martha said softly, 'you were only sixteen, still a child. Nothing I say will make you feel worse than your guilt and regret has done over the years and I don't want you to carry this remorse any longer. It's time to let go of it now. We didn't know two people were in the car but even if this Rob had let you go to Michael, it was almost certainly too late. There was nothing you could have done. Michael died instantly – I drew comfort from knowing it at the time – my husband didn't suffer. It wasn't until a couple of weeks later that I learned I was pregnant with Rachel, a timely comfort when I greatly needed it. My pregnancy was welcome news and in a small way Michael is still with me in Rachel.'

'But if I'd come forward and Rob had been brought to justice, wouldn't it have helped?' I asked.

'I'm not sure it would. Initially, anger at the unfairness of it unsettled me and I wanted someone to blame. But when the police investigation found nothing, I consciously decided to stop being angry – it was making me bitter, something I didn't wish to become. Rachel gave me a reason to go on living. She was part of Michael, his child, to bring up in a way which would have made him proud – anger and bitterness would have impeded that so I let it go. My daughter has been my life and now Rachel's given me two wonderful grandchildren to love and care for. Life's too precious to waste on negative emotions. And so you see, Helen, you've done everything possible to make amends and I appreciate your honesty and bravery. If you were in a similar situation today, I'm sure you'd act differently and do the right thing, but you were only a child and a frightened child.

'You have nothing to reproach yourself for, and now you must put it all behind you and enjoy the time you have left. Rachel tells me you have grandchildren, so make every minute with them count. If you need to know you are forgiven, then I forgive you and thank you for the steps you've taken to make this right.' Martha smiled at me. She was a remarkable woman, and the visit I'd dreaded finally released me from the guilt I'd carried for all those years.

We drank our coffee in relative silence with little attempt at polite conversation. Martha Walters had given me a wonderful gift in her generous words of forgiveness. Unfortunately, we would never see each other again, but this one meeting had lifted the dark cloud of guilt from my mind, for which I was grateful.

As the two women rose to leave, Martha stepped forward and hugged me. The scent of the delicate perfume she wore and her remarkable forgiveness lingered long after they left. I would do as she suggested and make these last weeks of my life count for something. I rang Luke, feeling better than I had for a long time, and asked him to come for me and take me to join in with my family's Christmas preparations.

THIRTY-FOUR
HELEN

3rd January

Christmas lived up to expectations, a warm and wonderful festival. It held so much more than previous years' celebrations have, particularly those Christmases since Andrew died, when festivities were forced – going through the motions for the children's sake.

Knowing this would be my last Christmas heightened the pleasure rather than detracting from it as I'd feared. But naturally, it was the boys who made it all so special. On Christmas Eve, I sat in my daughter's home, watching the excitement build in their eager faces. They giggled and whispered, sitting under the tree looking at the small pile of presents which friends had left for them, longing to open them but aware Father Christmas was watching and they must be good. It could have been Luke and Megan all those years ago – Christmas has always been such a special family time.

The tree was magnificent. We've never succumbed to artificial trees and the scent of pine coupled with the smell of baking from the kitchen injected an infectious excitement into the boys, encompassing even Gus. He thought their sole purpose in life was to play with him.

Boxes from my freezer were brought to Megan's house beforehand. The whole family enjoyed the selection of cakes and tray bakes, favourites throughout the years, which I'd baked to contribute to the festive preparations. I'd moved into Megan's house three days before Christmas, which allowed me to be in the midst of my family and part of the building excitement. Luke and Imogen continued to stay at my house but Ethan was now inseparable from Sam so they occupied his room while I took the spare bedroom. It worked well, and Megan took two weeks' leave to spend with us all.

As always, we went to church on Christmas Eve to a carol service. Admittedly we're not regular churchgoers, but we always wanted our children to know the true meaning of Christmas, so often buried beneath the presents and commercialism of the festivities. The service grounded us all, bringing a particular perspective into play. Our parish church offers a traditional service of nine lessons and carols, and the boys were delighted as the lights dimmed and we sat in candlelight to sing 'Away in a Manger', the only carol they knew.

Again, I resorted to using the wheelchair – I don't think I could have walked the short distance from the car to the church. After coffee and mince pies we greeted old friends, many of whom knew nothing of my illness and were visibly shocked by my appearance. I wished we were still in the subdued light of the candles. The vicar offered to visit me sometime soon, which I accepted, wanting to discuss funeral arrangements with him. On our return home I was as ready for bed as were my grandsons, and we all retired early in anticipation of a magical Christmas Day.

It did not disappoint. Father Christmas had been and the

boys eagerly tore open presents, far too many, but it was a special Christmas and I'd never again have the opportunity to spoil my family. Stockings were emptied of fruit and chocolate and Sam and Ethan were restrained from eating it all in case they couldn't manage Christmas dinner.

There were surprises for the adults, too – still my precious children. Imogen squealed when she opened the beautiful leather bag I'd bought for her. It was the kind of quality she would never buy for herself, which was precisely the point. James was surprised at the leather briefcase and thanked me profusely. Luke's iPad cover and leather wallet were also well received. I so enjoyed seeing their faces, particularly my grandsons, who received all they wanted and more besides. Another surprise was the tickets for the pantomime I'd purchased for them all. As they thanked me, I confided how it was the only way I could ensure a peaceful day, therefore a selfish gesture on my part! The tickets were for Boxing Day, the matinee performance and the day before Luke and Imogen would return to Canada, a day I dreaded.

Christmas dinner was nothing short of perfect, a traditional feast which suited each one of us. Megan and Imogen had worked together to provide a delicious meal, enthusiastically devoured by us all.

Although wanting to stay up all through Christmas Day, I succumbed to a short sleep after lunch. Resting on my bed, the sound of happy laughter from downstairs made me smile. Children make Christmas, and the boys and their parents enjoyed the day – a day I'm sure they'd remember for various reasons.

The pantomime proved a great success and my family arrived home with the usual jokes of, *oh yes he did, oh no he didn't,* making me laugh as they told me all about it, but my laughter was only half-hearted. Having promised myself I'd be strong when the time came for Luke and his family to return home, it was probably one of the hardest things I've ever had to do. There was no way I'd ever travel to visit them again and Luke had responsibilities; they needed to return home.

We sat up late that evening after the children went to bed. Having slept while everyone was at the theatre, I stayed awake longer than usual, hanging on to Luke's every word and delighted by the love I witnessed between him and Imogen. Megan would miss her brother when he left, and I felt for her, as again, she would be without her twin when facing one of the most challenging times of her life. Still, James was a rock who grounded her and supported my daughter in every way. When Luke and Imogen finally returned to my house for the last time, I went to bed.

Feeling tired is my new normal. Once alone, the tears I'd promised not to shed were finally released, selfish tears for all the things I would miss and all the things I'd never get to do. It was clear I'd not see much of the new year, if any at all. The hope of another few weeks was not to be.

Morning dawned as it must, and having slept fitfully, I went down to have breakfast with my grandchildren. They were still high from the pantomime, giggling over silly jokes and repeating the lines they could remember. After breakfast, Luke and Imogen arrived. I could see the rental car from the window, packed with much more than they'd brought, and I suddenly feared they might get charged for extra baggage because of all the things I'd given them. But what did something like that matter in the scheme of things, or was I filling my mind with trivia to avoid the main event? Luke held me in his arms for several moments when he arrived. We all thought the same thing, yet no one wanted to verbalise it.

This was the final parting.

We moved to the lounge to finish our coffee, and I asked the details of their journey. Luke knew they must leave shortly, the weather wasn't good and would probably delay them, but his reluctance was evident. Ethan climbed onto my knee and snuggled into me. Tired from the recent festivities he would probably sleep for most of the journey. I wrapped him in my arms and tried to store the feel of his slender body in my mind, another memory to replay later.

Time does not stand still, no matter how much we want it to, and the parting came. There were only a few last-minute things to squeeze into the car and then it was time to say goodbye. The boys clung to each other and to their respective aunt and uncle then Ethan kissed me before scrambling into the car. Imogen, with tears in her eyes, held on to me, thanking me for my generosity and saying she'd miss me before climbing into the passenger seat. Luke looked tearful as he hugged me close, whispering how much he loved me, words I echoed sadly – and then they were gone.

Back in the warmth of the house, I wondered how I could possibly bear this sadness and separation from those I loved so much. But the rhythm of the world continues, day following day, week following week, year following year – and will continue to do so for my family without my participation. Life is fleeting and being such, we must make every moment count.

When Luke left, so did much of my strength and determination. I have no more goals to strive for and remaining positive won't be easy during these last few weeks. My son rang later, to tell us they'd arrived safely at the airport and were waiting for their flight. Megan spoke to him briefly before passing the phone to me. I hardly knew what to say, but he promised to Skype when they were home the following day, and we said another uncomfortable farewell.

It was only after this call that I really noticed Megan's distress. She would miss her brother and another last farewell was moving closer each day. I mustn't be selfish and think only of myself. Megan, Sam and James were still with me and I must also think of them.

I'd booked a place at Saint Bartholomew's for later this month, although I'd not yet told my children. The latest visit to Mr Connors confirmed what I already knew: the cancer had spread rapidly and my time was running out. It's now an effort to do anything physical; even writing my journal proves difficult. I may not be able to write much more, but I want you to know how much I love you all.

I'll remain with Megan until the time comes. Gus has already made this his home, where he'll be loved and cared for.

Dearest Luke and Megan. My hope is that reading this is not too painful for you and you will not think harshly of me. Events and conversations have been recorded as accurately as I remember, but please forgive any rambling. My body is failing and I'm so tired. Death will truly be a release. My desire now is to be somehow reunited with Andrew. When together, we will watch our family grow and live their lives to the full.

THIRTY-FIVE
MEGAN

The journal must have been painful to write. It's so brutally honest. I only found and read this account after Mum's death, which is as she wished. Knowing how some entries would shock us, she still trusted us with them and I'm glad for such honesty. My mother was a flesh-and-blood human being who made mistakes, as we all do, and wouldn't wish to be remembered as some kind of saint. But, to her credit, Mum attempted to rectify past mistakes, a courageous thing to do and something from which many of us would shy away. For this courage I admire her immensely.

The journal offers a series of snapshots into Mum's life, freeze-frames if you like, of things I knew and some I did not. An account of Helen Reid's life in her own words – an account in which she bares heart and soul for those of us who are left to judge, or not, as seems fit. It's a journal in which bravery shines through, although Mum would certainly not agree!

Incredibly, Mum managed to do so much in those last few weeks and months of her life, a testament to her enduring strength of character. If I'd known what she was going through earlier, perhaps I could have helped, but typically, Mum wanted to protect me, to make my life as easy and carefree as possible.

On 15th January, Mum moved into the hospice where she'd chosen to spend her final days. When Luke returned to Canada, a part of Mum went with him. The knowledge she would never see her son again was a heavy burden to bear and her weariness grew more apparent with each passing day.

A huge part of me went with Luke, too – corny, I know, but it was like missing my right arm. Perhaps it's because we are twins that I felt the loss so keenly, but also because another loss was imminent and appeared to be coming sooner than we'd thought.

I noticed a change in Mum around the time she wrote about meeting Martha Walters. Before then, she fought hard, battling to keep going which I can now see was for a specific reason. After meeting Martha, it seemed as if she'd achieved her one last goal.

Mum didn't exactly give up on life but became more resigned to the inevitability of her death. More than once since Christmas, she told me she was ready to go; she was weary and knew it was time. Such words were delivered sensitively considering my feelings as Mum tried hard to make this easier for me. Now I can equate this change with what was going on in her life. I've gleaned from the journal that her fighting spirit was for a reason. I'm just so glad the meeting with Martha was beneficial.

It's hard to imagine your parent as a child or a teenager. We seem to think they've always been the same, yet this journal brought Mum's past life to the fore and gave Luke and me a rare opportunity to get to know the young Helen Reid or Helen Ross as she was then. I fully understand why she never told us about that very worst period in her life, but it would have made no difference to our love for her if she had.

Perhaps going to the police at the time would have been the right thing, but the fault lay with Rob Wheeler. Mum was also a victim of his bullying, and although it's taken years to achieve, I'm glad he will now be held accountable for his crimes.

The little room Mum occupied in the hospice was light and cheerful. A pot of scented hyacinths filled the room with perfume, and a soft lemon duvet added colour and warmth. When Mum finally came here to stay, the doctor told me she had only a matter of days left, perhaps a week if we were lucky. My first thought was of Luke. I rang to tell him, and as I'd hoped, my brother said he would be on the first available flight to England. When I told Mum, she smiled; having not expected to see Luke again, this news gave her something to stay strong for and hold on a little while longer.

I spent as much time as possible at the hospice. James looked after Sam to free my time, and the surgery where I worked was understanding and generously allowed me as long as I needed. The atmosphere at the hospice was incredible. The residential wing was at the opposite side of the building to the daycare facilities, but the sounds of music and laughter often drifted into the room, not a disturbance but a delight to hear. Staff popped in regularly to see if Mum or I needed anything, and the medication was monitored carefully and administered intravenously.

Mum drifted in and out of sleep, smiling when she opened her eyes to find me still there. I could hardly bear to leave.

Luke joined us within forty-eight hours of receiving my call, and I almost collapsed into his arms when he came through the door. It was evening, and he looked at Mum, who was sleeping, and then at me and instructed me to go home and sleep while he took up the vigil. Although reluctant to leave, I admitted my exhaustion and, conscious of the baby growing within me, I needed to be sensible, if only for her. I drove home to see my husband and son and rest my tired body.

Incredibly I slept for ten hours and awoke to an empty house. James's note on the kitchen table told me he'd taken Sam to nursery and gone to work. After a quick shower, I returned to Saint Bartholomew's, refreshed and feeling much better.

Mum was awake and talking to Luke, a smile on her pale face. They both turned to greet me and I garbled an apology for being away so long, which they both waved away, insisting I had needed the rest. I took my place on the opposite side of Mum's bed. She was somewhat brighter that morning, and her speech was clearer than it had been for the last few days, although still slightly laboured.

Luke insisted he'd slept on the plane and dozed at the bedside throughout the night, so he didn't need a break. He'd eaten breakfast in the dining room while the nurses bathed Mum and made her comfortable.

It was one of those situations when you didn't know what to discuss. Mum was clearly tired, yet trying to stay awake. Telling her to sleep was futile, so we talked about the children and Christmas, recalling recent events and chuckling over things the boys said and did. Since Christmas, Sam and Ethan had spoken to each other daily on Skype and it looked like their friendship would continue, which delighted us all. They were the next generation, the continuation of our family line.

Mum tired quickly, and soon her eyelids closed. We were holding hands across the duvet, forming a triangle, mother, son and daughter, when we became aware of a rasping sound in Mum's breathing, only for a minute or two before it stopped altogether, and she was gone.

THIRTY-SIX

MEGAN

The days after Mum's death revealed how much effort she'd put into sorting out her affairs to make our task as easy as possible, from instructions about the funeral, to precisely what she wished to happen to her earthly possessions.

Before the service, Mum wanted a private cremation to allow the family to say farewell at the crematorium. The service in the church afterwards would then celebrate her life.

The morning of the funeral dawned cold with a heavy frost, but dry. I've always hated funerals, especially winter ones when the weather made things much gloomier. It felt unreal as I stood, flanked by James and Luke, watching the coffin being carried in. The coffin was woven from what appeared to be willow, another decision Mum made herself, and I was glad things were being done as she wanted.

We were only in the crematorium for about twenty minutes, after which our little group found ourselves outside in the bitterly cold morning air with large snowflakes beginning to fall lightly. It wasn't enough to cover the ground but enough to remind me of when I was a little girl and snow had fallen in our garden. Mum wrapped us all up and we went outside to build a snowman. She later told me how every snowflake was unique and no two were the same, just like people. To me, it was such an amazing fact, and I spent the rest of the day cutting out endless paper snowflakes to see if I could make each one different – unique – just as we are.

We hurried to the car which would take us on to the next stage of the farewell. Mum had planned the service with the vicar, choosing her favourite readings and hymns. It was undoubtedly the only funeral I'd ever attended where 'Away in a Manger' was sung, and I was transported back to the carol service we attended in the same church just a few short weeks before. The thought of the boys singing together made me smile.

Mum had furnished the vicar with a potted history of her life, which he read almost word for word without embellishments or exaggeration as Mum had requested. Flowers were to be from the family only, with gifts instead to Saint Bartholomew's. Several of the staff from the hospice attended the service, and it was easy to pick out Claire, with her purple hair and whacky dress sense. Mum would have preferred us all to wear bright colours like Claire – it would have appealed to her sense of fun.

The church was packed, a testament to Mum's popularity. There was her group of close friends, 'The Ladies who Lunch' as I always thought of them, together with former employees, neighbours and a few people I couldn't place. One face I did recognise, however, was Rachel Amos. We'd met only once when I was at the hospital for my scan, but I recognised her beautiful red hair. After the service, a general invitation was given for all friends to linger in the church hall for refreshments.

Luke and I mingled among the mourners, thanking them for coming, accepting their condolences and sharing memories of our mother and, occasionally, our father. Imogen didn't come over for the funeral; she'd said goodbye after Christmas and there was no need to travel so far again.

As the mourners left and we were able to go home, I was exhausted. Luke drove me home while James went to the nursery for Sam. Luke would be returning home the following day and was apologetic for leaving me with everything to do. I told him just how much Mum herself had done to ease this time for us and reminded him that I had James to help. And so, the day after we said goodbye to Mum, I again said goodbye to my brother. Even though he'd be so many miles away, I knew he would be there for me when I needed him, and with the wonderful internet, we could even speak face to face.

Mum's journal was sometimes painful to read as it revealed parts of her life about which I'd known nothing, events that had caused her much pain over the years. Tears rolled down my face while reading it, and I felt the impossible urge to hug my mother close and comfort her, as she so often did for me. Reflecting on the worst of times, I felt her pain. Regret for not doing the right thing haunted Mum throughout her life, but her courageous steps to redeem herself during a time of illness and pain speak volumes of her character. Surely none of us can judge another unless we have walked in their shoes? I'm so proud of my mother for how she strived to right this wrong.

I will send the journal to Luke, together with Mum's letter. He, too, I'm sure, will find Mum's actions to be nothing short of credit to her. I've always been proud to call Helen Reid my mother and continue to do so.

The evening was drawing in and as I looked out the window, snow fell gently onto the garden in huge, unique flakes. Baby Helen turned within me, a gentle fluttering movement, and I pressed my hand over my growing child.

My gaze travelled towards the darkening sky where I imagined Mum and Dad together again and I whispered, 'I love you, Mum.'

The End

ALSO BY GILLIAN JACKSON

The Pharmacist

The Victim

The Deception

Abduction

Snatched

The Accident

The Shape of Truth

The Charcoal House

The Dead Husband

———

Remembering Ellie

Ask Laura

AUTHOR'S NOTES

Thank you for reading *A Measure of Time*. I hope you enjoyed following Helen's story, a tale of bravery and positivity in a dire situation.

One of the joys of writing is the attempt to delve into a character's mind, to walk in their shoes, so to speak. For those of us, like myself, who have crossed a certain threshold of age, we can reflect on the years with a mix of joy and regret, drawing wisdom from our individual life experiences. It is my hope that through this book, we have shared some of these unique experiences together.

To read more of my work, please visit my Amazon author page, or find me on Facebook @gillianjacksonauthor Follow me on Twitter @GillianJackson7 or visit my website: www. gillianjackson.co.uk

ACKNOWLEDGEMENTS

As always, I am grateful to my husband and family for their unwavering love and support during the countless hours I spend writing. And to the exceptional team at Bloodhound Books, your invaluable help in bringing this book to life is truly appreciated. Each book is a collaboration. I have the privilege of crafting characters and spinning plots, while you diligently work on the refining and presenting. Your dedication, professionalism, and guidance have been a great help throughout this process.

A NOTE FROM THE PUBLISHER

Thank you for reading this book. If you enjoyed it please do consider leaving a review on Amazon to help others find it too.

We hate typos. All of our books have been rigorously edited and proofread, but sometimes mistakes do slip through. If you have spotted a typo, please do let us know and we can get it amended within hours.

info@bloodhoundbooks.com

.

Milton Keynes UK
Ingram Content Group UK Ltd.
UKHW022115070624
443768UK00004B/92

9 781916 978980